THIS BOOK BELONGS TO

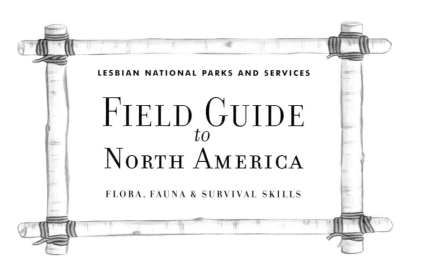

LESBIAN NATIONAL PARKS AND SERVICES

Field Guide
to
North America

FLORA, FAUNA & SURVIVAL SKILLS

by

RANGER SHAWNA DEMPSEY & RANGER LORRI MILLAN

Illustrations by Daniel Barrow

PEDLAR PRESS | TORONTO

PEDLAR PRESS
PO Box 26, Station P, Toronto Ontario M5S 2S6 Canada

ACKNOWLEDGEMENTS.
The publisher gratefully acknowledges the financial support
of the Canada Council for the Arts and the Ontario Arts
Council for its publishing program.

The artists gratefully acknowledge the support of the
Canada Council for the Arts.

NATIONAL LIBRARY OF CANADA CATALOGUING
IN PUBLICATION

Dempsey, Shawna
    Lesbian national parks and services field guide to
North America : flora, fauna and survival skills / Shawna
Dempsey and Lorri Millan.

ISBN 0-9686522-6-3

    1. Lesbianism — Humor. I. Millan, Lorri II. Title.

PN6231.L43D45 2002   C818'.5407   C2002-903519-8

First Edition

ILLUSTRATIONS Daniel Barrow
COPY-EDIT Adam Levin
DESIGN Zab Design & Typography
Typeset using Filosofia, designed by Zuzana Licko (Emigre)

Printed in Canada

To Anne Murray Canada's Songbird

Table of Contents

LESBIAN NATIONAL PARKS AND SERVICES

FIELD GUIDE
to
NORTH AMERICA

Preface

WELCOME TO THE *Lesbian National Parks and Services Field Guide to North America*, the first comprehensive compendium to the lesbian wilderness. In this slim volume we endeavour to provide you with all the information and survival skills necessary to enjoy your outdoor activities to the fullest. Whether you are a neophyte wayfarer or seasoned bushwoman, may these pages illuminate your path. Years of hands-on experience and meticulous research have contributed to this text and we are confident that this shared knowledge will arouse an unbridled passion for lesbianism in all its forms.

Common varieties of lesbian Flora and Fauna are herein described, along with facts of special note to the ardent woodswoman. This material is not arranged hierarchically, for we at Lesbian National Parks and Services (LNPS) take issue with ideas of primacy in nature. Although Latin names are provided for each species, even this system of nomenclature has been called into question for alluding to an obsolete, linear model of evolution, as opposed to a more accurate, web-like pattern. The history of biology has been negligent in acknowledging the full range of behaviour within a species, and particularly blind to lesbians. For eons, "Nature" and "The Natural" have been equated with retro-hetero mumbo-jumbo. But no longer! There is a whole world of lesbianism waiting to be studied and enjoyed! May this handbook be your guide.

We would be remiss if we did not extend a hearty thank-you to all the Junior Rangers whose life-lessons grace these pages. In this book you will meet but a fraction of the dynamic women who make up the Corps, inspiring us each and every day with their commitment, good grooming and bonhomie. When our courage and stamina falter, the thought of our Junior Rangers works like a healing balm upon our weary brows. Our deep bond with the membership of Lesbian National Parks and Services — more than sisters, more than friends — is strengthened with each step we take into the fascinating, challenging and sometimes even treacherous lesbian wilds.

Unfortunately, the confines of space have forced us to focus upon North American lesbians. We trust that our readership in Oceania, Africa, Asia, Europe and South America will find much of the material transferable to their own rich ecosystems. Although lesbian species vary from region to region, the methodology for experiencing them remains the same. This Field Guide will prove helpful in negotiating the complexity of lesbian form and behaviour wherever you may find it. But let caution prevail. If you find yourself in a particularly sticky situation, remember, "Safety first." That said, it is important that all who read this book, be they casual lesbian observers or eager Ranger recruits, approach it with a spirit of willing adventure.

Walk with us awhile! Spend some time in our hiking shoes or in our tents. And remember, wherever you live and wherever you may roam, let the Golden Rule of Lesbian National Parks and Services be your guide: *Do unto lesbians as you would have lesbians do unto you.*

— Ranger SHAWNA DEMPSEY and Ranger LORRI MILLAN
   Winnipeg, Canada, June 2002.

Introduction

1

THIS BOOK IS MORE than a manual to North American lesbiancraft, it is a paean to variation and deviation. We hope that this testament to diversity will inspire, as you navigate the many twisted trails of lesbianism wherever they may lead.

Nature, in all Her bounty, holds the templates for myriad choices. It is up to us to look beyond clichés and supposition – to delve deeply into science – and open our eyes to the resplendent variety which surrounds us. If we do, perhaps we shall have the courage to follow the example of millions of different plant and animal species and to pursue our natural desires to their natural conclusions.

We ought not to forget that we ourselves are an integral part of Nature. Though we have oft failed in our role as stewards, our bestial instinct for survival (as exemplified by our need for sex, food, water and shelter) unites us with other creatures of the planet. Fish, fowl, fruit, mammal, microbe, moss: each has a particular bent which fulfills Nature's design and contributes to the interwoven fabric of life. Likewise, every individual within a species, whatever their idiosyncrasies, furthers the evolutionary process by testing the bounds of what is possible and efficacious.

Biology, as revealed in this Field Guide, dismisses monolithic models (such as heterosexuality and patriarchy) and encourages a perversion of norms. It is only through plurality that any species, including our own, will continue to evolve. Herein lies the challenge for the ardent lesbian-lover. It is simply this: observe, experience, experiment and do not judge. Nature awaits within each of us. By studying Her many manifestations throughout the North American continent, may we also learn about ourselves.

The Story of
Lesbian National Parks and Services

UNTIL THE FORMATION of Lesbian National Parks
and Services we, Founding Rangers Shawna Dempsey
and Lorri Millan, were not unlike many readers
of this Field Guide: avid woodswomen with a
passion for biology. However, despite our bound-
less outdoor enthusiasm, we had long experienced
frustration in the bush. With each dogged step into
the wilds it became increasingly clear that, without
the support of scientists or conservation officials and,
in fact, ignored by wildlife professionals in general,
lesbian Flora and Fauna had been left to wither and
decline, surviving mainly in isolated communities
largely invisible to the casual observer. This official
indifference frustrated us. We knew well the rewards of careful observation and patient tracking,
and had uncovered hidden worlds of lesbian activity
in even the most inhospitable environments. These
communities were particularly vulnerable to changes
in political climate and unnatural disasters such as
religious fundamentalism and assimilation. Sadly,
lesbianism was operating far from its peak potential.
Even when confronted with this problem, most con-
servationists responded blankly. Try as we might,
we could not prevail upon park wardens or wildlife
officials to act.

Impassioned concern often kept us awake long into the night. Warm in our camprolls, serenaded by the haunting call of the loon and the lonely, grey she-wolf, we were plagued by basic questions of species survival. Surely something must be done. But what? If only the fragile lesbian ecosystem was given the attention required to encourage proliferation! If only a force of trained professionals could turn its vigilant gaze on the plight of the lesbian wilds! And if only, in doing so, these do-gooders could inspire tidiness and good grooming amongst their followers!

These thoughts fermented in our minds, like a yeast culture growing into feverish bloom. By the spring of 1997, it was an itch that demanded scratching! In June of that year, we embarked upon a fateful bushwalk. In many ways it was like other forays into lesbianism, although on this occasion thwarted desire transformed the junket into a fountainhead of change. We were particularly unsatisfied, having spent a long day tracking the elusive lesbian moose through the dense forests of the Great Canadian Shield. However, our disappointment did not sour our spirits and, indeed, seemed to have the opposite effect. In the waning firelight our eyes glowed, radiating steely resolve and indomitable courage. "What if ", we wondered aloud, "*we* were to form an organization dedicated to lesbian wildlife?" The time was nigh, we realized, to take matters into our own hands.

With vigour and excitement we set about creating a service entrusted with the stewardship of all lesbian life forms. This needed to be a force strong enough to stand up against species tyranny, while at the same time imbued with sufficient leadership qualities to promote the lesbian way. The rank and file of the organization would have to be more than merely scientifically curious. Their involvement must be a calling, answered with the same passion with which we replied to the call of the errant bull-dyke Moose that fateful night in the Canadian northland. Only the finest woodswomen, driven by a desire to right wrongs, to help others and to touch and be touched by a plethora of needy lesbians, would embark on a mission so wide-ranging and so all-consuming. The task was daunting but, like all great movements, it began with a single gesture born of great conviction: the donning of a uniform.

As we buttoned ourselves into crisp shirts and trousers of tan, we understood the pride of being a Lesbian Ranger, and the joy of dedicating ourselves to the betterment of all lesbiankind.

Hence, Lesbian National Parks and Services was born.

Founding Foremothers

A Life More Than a Lifestyle

MANY PASSERSBY seem startled by their encounter with the Lesbian Rangers. Perhaps they are struck dumb by the sight of so many man-made fibres put to such a handsome use; perhaps they are amazed that this valiant Force was not founded sooner; perhaps they are merely grateful that at long last Sapphic species are being given their due. Whatever emotions might fill their breasts, their mouths do not remain agape for long and invariably they queery, "What, exactly, do you do?" Though a rather forward question, it is almost always met with a good-natured chuckle. In fact, there is very little that the Lesbian Ranger has not experienced, beating the bushes day-in, day-out, in hot pursuit of lesbian wildlife. She loves her job. And yet this intrepid veteran of the wilds is sometimes saddened by the magnitude of lesbian need, as it far outstrips her available resources. This is why Lesbian National Parks and Services developed a three-pronged approach of education, research and recruitment to most effectively serve and service the vast and varied lesbian ecosystem. While remaining flexible to hitherto unimagined situations, the Force focuses upon these most pressing needs, to the benefit of all.

EDUCATION

Nothing is more satisfying than watching a child's
eyes light up as a lesbian scurries out from beneath
the leaf mould. All of us take pleasure in the beauty
of plants and animals in their natural habitat. The
complexity, grace and finely tuned coexistence of every
living thing teaches us, young and old alike, respect
for our environment and for each other as well.

The Lesbian Ranger's fieldwork allows for frequent contact with the general public, and ample
opportunity to elucidate the lessons that nature so
eloquently teaches. Coupled with LNPS literature,
these brief but meaningful encounters do much to
enlighten all who meet the Ranger. Various lesbians
are pointed out to the wayfarer, along with tips on
how best to approach the specimen. Fascinating
facts and environmental cautions are also imparted,
further edifying the listener.

Most importantly, all who see the Lesbian
Ranger, neat and trim in green and tan, learn about
courage. Her physical presence serves as a symbol
and reminds us that camouflage, though useful
in the short term, does not ensure long-term survival. The jaunty Ranger instructs us, by example, to
be visible, to assert our territory, and never, ever to
forget that lesbianism is an essential part of any
community.

RESEARCH

The diversity of lesbian behaviour is truly limitless. However, the uninitiated eye can be blind to this bounty. Fortunately, the LNPS Ranger is a tireless professional well-versed in lesbian organisms. No creature is too small and no gesture too insignificant to escape the penetrating gaze of the Force. Data is amassed, checked and double-checked. But the work does not stop there. Lesbian National Parks and Services uses this information to make more informed decisions about habitat preservation, culling and the tricky business of lesbian reproduction. Primary research has been carried out in all areas where the Rangers have been posted, and the results of these ground-breaking studies are being used to sustain and increase lesbian populations. The Ranger's work with lesbian seagulls, for example, has garnered worldwide attention, and has earned respect for this once maligned seabird. Our feathered friends no longer are considered mere scavengers, but handsome sailors: traversing oceans, tidying waterfronts and co-parenting hatchlings in all-female rookeries. As the seagull illustrates, understanding a lesbian species (what they eat, where they live, when and with whom they sleep) leads to appreciation, better resource management and a happier, healthier world for all.

RECRUITMENT

Lesbian National Parks and Services has made great strides in the fields of education and science, but there is still so much to be done. That is why the Rangers not only encourage the proliferation of all lesbian species but also actively seek new members to admit into its folds. Lesbian National Parks and Services provides opportunities to excited and adventuresome women of all ages, of all abilities and of all commitment levels.

Some potential recruits may be willing to embrace what is more than a lifestyle, and embark upon the LNPS vocation. Others, though consumed with a heartfelt desire to serve the Rangers, may not have sufficient time or stamina and may consider joining the LNPS Reserve, which is called upon in times of great need. Others still may want to get involved with the Junior Lesbian Rangers. These strapping women, be they young or simply young-at-heart, learn the basics of lesbiancraft while enjoying fulfilling friendship and outdoor fun.

Community organizing is essential to the growth of LNPS and the achievement of its goals. Recruitment, long a lesbian survival strategy, is the most successful method of swelling the ranks and ensuring that this valuable work continues to the benefit of all lesbian species, and to the larger ecosystem as well. As you read these pages, consider how you might want to become involved.

Getting Started

2

So MANY WOMEN WISH they could experience the lesbian wilds. Little do they know, it is so easy! All it takes is one bold step on life's bushpath, and within no time they are inveterate woodswomen. They may be nervous at first but, once they begin, it comes so naturally they wonder what took them so long to get started.

Truly, all great journeys begin with a single step. Whether you prefer to observe from a distance or dive in with both hands, lesbianism has so much to offer. It would be a shame to let its bounty pass you by. Just ask some of the excitable women who make up the Junior Ranger Corps. Why, the eager beavers of Peterborough 4th Division go to bed while the sun still shines and are up and at 'em before day-break, simply so they can maximize their time in the bush! In the words of J.R. Jean Brophey, "Each day brings new discoveries and new challenges. My outdoor activities have pushed me far beyond what I thought I was capable of, and taught me things I'd never dared imagine! Really, the tutelage I've received across Mother Nature's knee has made me the disciplined recruit I am today ".

J.R. Brophey and her chums in the Kawartha Lakes district have developed enviable endurance. Nonetheless, they would be the first to advise the lesbian tenderfoot that the duration is less important than the quality of the expedition. Start slowly. Your stamina will build, and within no time you will be ready for overnight adventures. However, before you embark upon even the shortest trail hike, learn the basics of bush-lore, so that your time will be well spent. A few easy-to-acquire skills and simple considerations will ensure that the experience is rewarding for you and others who might come later.

Comportment in the Bush

EARLY ONE SPRING morning, Junior Ranger Su Goldfish set out to explore the lovely Rocky Mountains of Canada's Banff National Park. She hummed a cheerful tune as she walked, eager to see the peaks of the beautiful Three Sisters. A few short kilometres into the bush, however, the Junior Ranger pulled up short. In a small clearing next to a babbling spring lay an abandoned campsite. Approaching with caution, J.R. Goldfish noted numerous herbal tea bags, a discarded Birkenstock insole, and crumpled wrappings from gluten-free snacks. This debris had been scattered willy-nilly about a still-smouldering campfire. Although the smell of stir-fry hung heavy in the air, the site was clearly abandoned. Automatically, the young naturalist piled earth onto the warm coals of the fire and gathered the garbage into her own waste bag. Sadly, shaking her tousled curls, she continued on her way, her load and her heart a little heavier than short moments before. "It is amazing", she reflected, "how a few untrained, gluten-free lesbians can spoil everyone's fun." So true, Junior Ranger Goldfish, so true!

Few among us can resist the lure of uncharted territory and the promise of its natural bounty. We are drawn, magnetically, mysteriously, away from our man-made lives into something larger than ourselves, something that speaks to an ancient yearning and touches us deep within. Call it "the wilds", "the country" or "the great outdoors": to the avid woodswoman it is simply "home". Nature awaits, be it for an evening, a weekend or months at a time. All she asks in return is that we tread softly and do no harm.

Being a good citizen in the wilds is of utmost importance. Good manners, erect posture and a sunny smile ought not be left at home. The same courtesies we offer to our softball teammates or bathhouse buddies should also be extended to our feral friends. Let common sense and concern for others prevail, and you will be well rewarded.

That said, while we are in Mother Nature's playground certain other rules of conduct apply. First and foremost, our presence should neither damage the environment nor leave evidence of our passing. While wayfaring in the wilderness you are a guest in the home of other species and should behave yourself accordingly. Here are a few simple rules to keep in mind while exploring virgin woods, shooting surging rapids or climbing perky promontories. They will ensure that your outdoor adventure will not adversely affect any who follow in your footsteps, be they lesbians great or small, wild or tame.

- Do not wear perfumes or highly scented products.
- Clear the area around your firepit of dry tinder.
- Before sleeping, tie foodstuffs from the high limb of a tree to avoid attracting mammals of other species.
- Thoroughly extinguish fires before breaking camp.
- Bury your excrement.
- Carry out all trash, including menstrual products.

As Junior Ranger Goldfish can attest, these very basic rules will make your forays into the wilderness more pleasurable for everyone and will preserve the wilds for generations to come.

Attire

JUNIOR RANGERS THE WORLD over have learned the value of being appropriately dressed for each and every occasion. These intrepid adventurers look "at-home" in any ecosystem, partly because of their well-chosen togs: easy-care polycotton has taken these outdoorswomen far! Certainly no one has ever accused them of being merely "fashionable" and, by following their example, you, too, will never meet that fate.

While tromping Cape Breton's Cabot Trail, Junior Ranger Belinda Allen is never without hooded rainwear. But if, perchance, she were to forget it, she knows that she can improvise a stylish poncho from the trash bag she carries at all times. Belted with a serviceable rope (always at the ready!) and filled with dry leaves, this trash-bag-cum-rain-shell is transformed into an insulated waistcoat, should the weather turn truly nasty.

Similarly, in quite a different ecosystem, Junior Ranger Rachel Melas doffs her shirt and tie at the Michigan Womyn's Big Game Park. She knows that to fully participate in the Game Park's bounty, a bare-breasted approach is more rewarding. Sun-block has been generously applied by a sister Ranger, a brimmed hat protects her from heatstroke and a canteen is strapped firmly to her belt.

Rachel always packs water and is happy to share her fluids. She knows the danger that dehydration poses for any active girl-on-the-move.

Whatever your mission, follow these sterling examples and let no-nonsense practicality and forethought be your guide. Whether your travails lead you through violently rough waters or quietly violent suburbs, you will look and feel your best if clad in wrinkle-free, serviceable clothing. Stout footwear, twill trousers, a proper visor and inclement-weather gear are not only attractive, but offer much-needed protection from the elements and may even make the difference between wilderness survival and death. Research the environment: the terrain and weather conditions. Anticipate problems and rise to the challenge! Keep in mind that your clothing should provide maximum comfort and mobility during the day *and* suitable warmth should you be forced to spend the night.

Form and function meet in the trash-bag poncho

When building an outfit, start from the bottom up. Underwear forms the foundation of any ensemble, and should be chosen for practical and aesthetic reasons, as well as personal inclinations. Fishnet garments worn next to the skin create an air-conditioning layer which allows the body to cool by evaporation of body heat. They are an excellent choice for hot, dry climes. However, when worn under a close-fitting garment in colder conditions, they provide valuable insulation. Similarly, silk stockings under wool socks are terrific insulators. Many woodswomen enjoy wearing this apparel or delight in seeing it on others.

Whatever your tastes, remember that layering is the key to success. It creates pockets of air that help regulate body heat. Garments can be added and subtracted as the situation dictates. Velcro fasteners expedite this process and are invaluable when timing is critical.

Where possible, choose items that do double duty. No doubt there are more tools at your fingertips than you realize. Creativity is the key.

■ A RAIN PONCHO also serves as a groundsheet. On even the shortest expeditions, there might be opportunities to lie down. Strung between trees, the poncho can also form a makeshift tent, perfect for impromptu overnight adventures. If need be, it can be used to create an evaporation still or transpiration bag to gather drinkable water.

■ USE A CLEAN white handkerchief as a ventilation mask during unexpected volcanic eruptions or, if it is dipped in vinegar, to lessen the effects of tear gas. (Occasionally, Lesbian Rangers encounter hostile, rival forces intent on preserving an unhealthy heterosexual status quo.) A hankie also comes in handy as a heat-reflective hat. And do not forget traditional uses. A white handkerchief is a nose-blower and a flag of surrender. Folded or twisted, it forms a sling, a bandage or a tourniquet.

■ A SHORT LENGTH of cord or twine has almost innumerable uses, as a fashion item or an implement. In a pinch, boot laces are adequate substitutes. Lash poles together to form a teepee support or make a noose to snare prey. Your belt is also a versatile tool. Do not limit it to keeping up your pants.

■ MANY VALUABLE ITEMS can be carried inside your shorts. This style of packing can be used to protect valuables or simply enhance your presence in the bush.

■ SILK STOCKINGS, as described above, are great insulators when worn under socks. They can also be used to strain water and even pan for gold. Whether used for warmth or prospecting, they are highly effective. Many a Junior Ranger, from Yukon's goldfields to California's hills, has used them to get lucky.

These are but a few examples from which you may draw inspiration. It is up to you to be imaginative and be prepared. Pack lightly and efficiently for the conditions of a given environment. Learn from Junior Rangers Allen and Melas and always dress "smartly" for the occasion.

Gear

Gear, like attire, should be chosen to withstand the rigours of your activity and the environment. Weight and bulk are important considerations. As woodswomen everywhere can attest, "Bigger is not always better" (although it is sometimes nice!). Aim for efficiency that reflects the demands of your situation.

Whatever the terrain and season, whether you embark on an extended tour or a brief junket, be sure to *always* take along a small basic kit. You never know when it might come in handy; you never know when it might save your life. The wilderness is a capricious mistress. Always be prepared.

BASIC KIT

water-tight, crush-proof container	Protect your camp essentials in one easy-to-locate container.
flint and striker	A reliable tool to create sparks, time after time.
waterproof matches	Can always be counted on to light a fire when all else fails.
candle	Provides light, minimal warmth and romantic ambiance.
compass	Assists confirmation of orientation.

topographic map of region	Make sure it is detailed and as up to date as possible.
water purification supplies	Available as tablets or in liquid iodine form.
large plastic trash bag	Provides shelter or rainwear. Also use to collect water and to carry trash.
multi-blade knife	Invaluable multi-purpose tool. Can cut food, firewood, shelter supports and restraints. Knives can include handy items such as eating utensils, can openers, corkscrews, scissors, tweezers, toothpicks and nail files.
small flashlight	Aids visibility at night and can be used to signal.
compact mirror	Helps maintain personal appearance. Excellent for signalling.

Always stow an extra pair of socks and a lightweight pullover in your rucksack. No matter how short your foray, carry a first-aid kit (see page 75). Bush conditions change rapidly, so be ready for quick chills and spills.

Also pack snacks and water to maintain your energy level. Chocolate, dried fruits and nuts provide high caloric value and are easy to carry. Other foodstuffs, such as cucumbers, zucchini and Chinese eggplant often come in handy. Remember, even the most intrepid outdoorswoman sometimes feels at a loss in the lesbian wilderness. However, she does not panic if she has a few well-chosen supplies that make her happily self-sufficient.

Camping stores carry a dizzying array of tents, stoves, sleeping bags and backpacks. Consider the merits of these products carefully, keeping in mind the particulars of your expedition. Store personnel and consumer guides are fonts of information. Be creative with your research! Junior Ranger Nadin Gilroy chose to pursue an older, more experienced woodswoman to help her assess her needs. The elder's eagerness to share surprised and pleased J.R. Gilroy and she has continued her inquiry to this day.

Whatever your circumstances and proclivities, keep your burden to a minimum. Your pack should never exceed one-quarter of your body weight and should be worn as high as possible on your shoulders. Many a fine lesbian has been laid low by back problems. Do not let this happen to you! Pack lightly, bend at the knees and support awkward positions with slings, straps and helping hands. Go forth into the bush equipped but not laden down with excessive baggage.

Lesbian Survival Skills

3

WHETHER TRAVERSING TURBULENT tributaries, trail-blazing temperate rainforests or tromping to the traditional watering hole, mastery of a few essential skills can mean the difference between a successful sortie and one filled with frustration, or even disaster. This section is devoted to imparting the knowledge necessary to achieve a full and rewarding experience in the lesbian wilds. In the main, this information will enrich your time in the bush. But we would be neglectful if we did not include advice for the adventurer who finds herself in trouble.

Junior Ranger Jill Town, a wily veteran of the wild, rightly points out that even the most experienced bushwoman will find herself, at some point in her life, lost. Whether it be for a few minutes or a few days, the ease with which one can step off even a well-trod trail and find oneself disoriented begs for an understanding of the basics of lesbian survival.

At LNPS, these skills are not limited to the essentials of fire- and shelter-building. They also include the oft-overlooked cornerstone of survival: lesbian psychology (see page 83). Remember, the lesbian mind is a powerful tool, if its energies are harnessed and focused upon practical matters executed with a sunny heart! Psychology, coupled with hands-on know-how like knot-tying, lesbian signals and what and whom to eat, prepare novice and expert alike for all eventualities and bestow the confidence needed to survive in this lesbian-eat-lesbian world.

Shelter

WITHOUT PROTECTION FROM the elements (cold, heat, wind and sun), long-term and, at times, short-term survival is virtually impossible. Fortunately, lesbians' superior nesting ability has long been noted by scientists and naturalists alike. Whatever the environment, lesbians excel at home-making. Snow shelters are easily constructed from snow blocks or dug out into cozy snow caves. Forests provide abundant materials to construct lean-to shelters or more enduring huts. In most situations one can improvise a tent using various items such as space blankets or clothing draped over tree limbs or rocks or even directly over one's body. With a little ingenuity, the possibilities are as varied as the lives they protect.

Expertise at shelter-building is widely believed to be the key to outdoor comfort, but years of obser-vation at LNPS have shown that successful lesbian nesting depends not on the nature of the shelter itself, but rather the quality of the bed within.

Over the years resourceful Junior Ranger Nikki Forrest had become expert at constructing pitch-perfect, weatherproof lean-tos, A-frames and quinzies. She understood that two or more bodies co-bedding improves morale, increases comfort and produces heat. However, she failed to grasp the reason why her immaculate shelters did not attract cohabitants. In contrast, her best trail-buddy, Junior Ranger Anne Golden, built rudimentary shelters that always played hostess to long lines of eager outdoorswomen. The consistent popularity of Anne's simple, near-tumble-down abodes puzzled J.R. Forrest. The mystery was finally solved when she got a closer look at Anne's queen-sized survival mattress.

J.R. Anne Golden struck upon her innovation after years of arduous lesbian experience and is eager to spare others needless hardship. She shares, "There are countless ways you can bed down in the great outdoors. True, the experienced bushwoman can dig hollows for her shoulders and hips and lay down on the ground and fall asleep, but that is not exactly an *inviting* scenario. On the other hand, a fragrant bed of luxurious evergreen boughs, carefully arranged for maximum suspension, turns a rough shelter into a five-star hotel. Like all members of the Junior Lesbian Corps, I try to live my life with the well-being of others uppermost in my mind and heart. I cannot, in good conscience, turn away a comfort-seeker. I do my best to accommodate all comers".

On wet ground, J.R. Golden starts with a platform of logs or sticks and then builds up layer after layer of boughs, grasses, ferns and other soft vegetation. If the ground is dry the platform is optional.

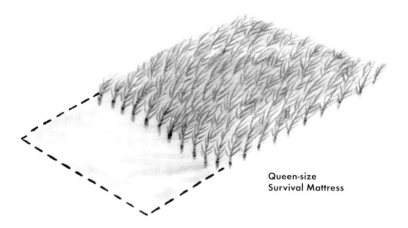

**Queen-size
Survival Mattress**

(*See diagram*.) Anne concludes, "If it seems like a lot of extra effort, keep in mind that it pays off in a mattress better suited to vigorous use and provides real comfort to weary lesbian bones".

    J.R. Golden's masterful attention to the details of wilderness shelters has not only protected her from the discomfort of the elements but has kept at bay many of the afflictions that have commonly plagued would-be survivors, such as backache and so-called lesbian bed-death. This lesson in creature comforts teaches us the value of prioritizing both physical and psychological health in the service of lesbian survival.

Keeping Wet

"DEHYDRATION IS THE ENEMY!" shouts an enthusiastic group of young Junior Rangers.

"Exactly," responds team leader J.R. Jenny Robinson. "All living things are composed primarily of water. Keeping wet in the wild is essential for the continued healthy functioning of the human body."

No Junior Ranger enters the bush without first mastering the skills that keep one's whistle wet. Finding or manufacturing safe drinking water comes second only to shelter in importance for the roaming lesbian. We must each consume three litres of H_2O a day and, while we can live for weeks without food, lesbians can survive mere days without replenishing lost liquids.

Even in the most arid environments, moisture can be found. In North America, water is rarely too far afield. There are a few simple methods for slaking your natural thirst. Use them alone or in combination to ensure that you and your buddies avoid the debilitating discomforts of dryness.

FREE-FLOWING SOURCES

Freshwater springs are fast flowing water courses which often can be found feeding into larger streams and rivers. They are located above the water they merge with and, when followed to their source (usually a crevice in a hillside), they reward the adventurer with almost limitless pure water. This water has been filtered through tons of great Mother Earth herself and, as a result, is delicious and untainted. Beyond the fountainhead, however, it becomes vulnerable to runoff, pollution and parasites.

PRECIPITATION

Always be prepared to collect rainwater. It is a fairly clean, trouble-free source of drinking water. Use any waterproof material to construct a raincatcher: rain ponchos, trash bags, rubber sheets or space blankets are ideal. Dental dams, while diminutive, work in a pinch. Locate or dig a depression in the land and line it with your impermeable sheath. This well can easily hold litres of water.

Snow is also a relatively safe, plentiful water source, but never eat it frozen. In cold conditions, always imbibe warmed beverages, as consuming cold drinks makes the body work harder and burns valuable calories.

DO DEW!

Collecting dew is another water-gathering possibility. In even the driest conditions water vapour condenses on ground, vegetation and rocks as the night air cools. Dewfall is most copious between 3:00 AM and sunrise, making this the ideal time for collection.

Lay a fully clad woman on low-lying grass or rocks, wait until she is soaked and then remove all her clothing. She will be grateful. Wring the wet fabric into a container. You will be amazed at how much moisture you have gathered. Repeat the procedure.

GETTING DOWN

Digging for water can be an effective approach in boggy territory. Dig a hole 30 cm deep and let the water seep in. Empty the hole a few times until the water becomes clear, then collect, purify (see page 54) and drink it. You can also dig holes next to a body of water and allow the separating soil to filter the water for you (purification is still required).

On a saltwater beach, dig above the high-tide mark. Whatever freshwater is present in the sand will seep into the hole and sit on top of the heavier saltwater.

Natural Filtration

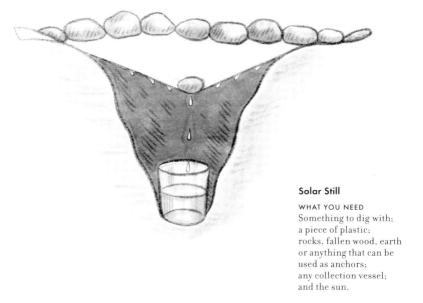

Solar Still

WHAT YOU NEED
Something to dig with;
a piece of plastic;
rocks, fallen wood, earth
or anything that can be
used as anchors;
any collection vessel;
and the sun.

DISTILLATION

Perhaps the most ingenious yet simple way to manufacture H_2O is the solar still. As the name suggests, by harnessing the radiant heat of the sun you can extract moisture from the soil using the simplest of tools.

The beauty of this method is that, by keeping a hole wet, one can distil an almost endless supply of condensed H_2O. Waste nothing! Pour used cooking and cleaning water into the bottom of your hole, cover it up and watch the sun do its work. In fact,

LESBIAN SURVIVAL SKILLS

any liquid, fetid or not, will be rendered absolutely pure through the miracle of liquid vapour condensation. Use your imagination. Try urine! Dig several holes and keep them all wet.

This brilliant process can provide a litre of water a day and works in any environment, including at sea. Instead of digging a hole, use a large bowl. Place seawater (or urine) in the bottom, a cup in the centre, cover with plastic and place a weight on the plastic over the cup. The end product is delicious. Enjoy!

PURIFICATION

Whatever method of water collection you use, it is wise to err on the side of caution. Even the toughest bushwhacker can be laid low by the tiniest of microbes, making it impossible to accomplish other tasks necessary for survival.

Water obtained from lakes, ponds, rivers, streams or bogs should be filtered and purified. Hold a cotton cloth over the mouth of your canteen as you submerge it. Flannel, long a lesbian favourite, works best. When the canteen stops bubbling, it is full.

Purification can be achieved via four methods:

■ Boil water for 5 minutes. (Important: remember that the boiling point of water lowers as elevation increases. In alpine locations put a lid on the pot to make sure the water gets really hot. Purification requires temperatures of at least 100°C.)

- Add 2–3 drops of liquid iodine to your canteen. Let stand 20 minutes.
- Use a commercially available water filter.
- Use a solar still.

If the water source smells fetid, is discoloured or foamy, do not use it. (Or distill using a solar still.)

Rule of Thumb: In this, as in other circumstances, minimize risk while still ensuring that your needs are met.

Fire

A RAGING FIRE is essential for comfort and camaraderie. Whether you are surviving sub-zero temperatures or making a sizzling meal to share with bosom buddies, building a fire and keeping it hot is a skill well worth perfecting. Junior Ranger Carol Philipps shares her campfire passion, "My fires always burn brightly, attracting all kinds of nocturnal lesbians. While I enjoy my solo forays in the bush, I also appreciate these nighttime visitors. They seek warmth and nourishment and, as a Junior Lesbian Ranger, I am happy to provide".

The following are descriptions of rudimentary fire-building techniques. But do not forget basic safety precautions. Pick a site well clear of overhanging trees. Clean the area of all flammable debris. Build a containment ring of rocks or a small trench full of water. Most importantly, never leave a campsite without drowning your fire with plenty of water or smothering it with sand or soil. It is inexcusable to walk away from a lesbian fire, no matter how cold it appears to be, without first ensuring that it is irrevocably extinguished. While these safeguards can be tedious, creating safe boundaries for your campfire fun will give you greater freedom in building a blaze that sparks, catches and roars excitedly all through the night.

FROM SPARK TO FLAME

Become expert at packing and you should be able to start a fire using the contents of your pockets. Whether you prefer a steel and flint, strike-anywhere matches or a magnifying glass, pay close attention to that first moment, when enough heat is generated to produce a pre-cious first spark. Without it there can be no fire, often with dire results on a cold night in the bush.

Some rough-and-ready ad-venturers prefer the challenge of hands-on combustion and have mastered age-old fire-starting techniques. For example, resourceful Junior Ranger Rachel Stone generates a flame using old-fashioned friction, with nothing more

Bow Drill

than four pieces of wood, her Junior Ranger pocket knife and a length of cord (which all Rangers, young and old, carry at all times). "I have always liked doing things with my hands and I love the challenge of making sparks fly on a frigid night", enthuses J.R. Stone. Her preferred approach to fire-making is the bow drill method, which comes alive in her practised hands.

Rachel advises, "Number one, never spare the lube! Pile it on and rub it in. You want that stick to spin in your hand while creating friction down below. Number two, have patience. Sparks don't fly instantly. Your drill needs time to do its work. The more you push and pull your bow the hotter things get. Relax into that back-and-forth rhythm and enjoy the heat before the fire".

Obviously, J.R. Stone has had much opportunity to perfect her style. However, the Junior Ranger's dexterity should not intimidate a novice. Excited sparks are within the grasp of even a fumbling amateur. If at first you do not succeed, keep trying. Perseverance can compensate if technique is lacking.

THE CLASSIC PYRAMID FIRE

This is a good, all-round fire. Once you have created a spark, you may need to gently fan the flames. Do not hurry the moment. Only after your tinder has caught and is burning with a steady heat should you make further moves and add more fuel to the fire.

The most common mistake the novice bushwhacker makes is building this fire too big. An inferno has the satisfaction of much drama and intense heat, but it lacks the subtlety and staying power of a small fire. Experienced outdoorswomen make fire with as little fuel as possible, building an efficient blaze. In this way they conserve energy and are able to burn brightly through many long and heated nights.

Whatever your methodology, play safely. There are few lesbians who have never been burnt. Use prudence and forethought and you will be sure to ignite with satisfaction.

Pyramid Fire

What and Whom to Eat

SATISFYING YOUR HUNGER is an urgent concern in the bush. An unsated appetite can seriously incapacitate the wilderness traveller. Be forearmed with the appropriate tools and information.

Food comes in all manner of packaging. It can be bought preserved in tins or dehydrated in foil packets. You can create your own rations in different sorts of carrying containers. Careful consideration should be given to the duration of your journey, the amount of weight that you can comfortably carry, whether you will augment your pack food with found foods as well as your own personal likes and dislikes.

J.R. Michelle Morrison does not like to disturb her surroundings when on the trails. Always thinking of others, she is happiest to observe and enjoy her environment rather than interfere with its delicate balance. She takes care to meet all her nutritional needs by carrying in her own favourite whole foods. Michelle says, "I love simple, delicious things like oatmeal with dried apricots, curried lentils or rice and beans".

According to J.R. Morrison, sharing is half the fun. "I'm an outgoing person who really enjoys getting to know my fellow nature-lover. There are always enough tofu dogs and hot biscuits to satisfy whomever I might chance upon." And indeed, who can resist her offerings!

Weenies and Biscuits

COMBINE
2 fistfuls of flour
2 two-finger pinches of salt
2 three-finger pinches of baking powder
1 two-finger blob of fat

Add just enough water to make a stiff
batter. Mix well. Shape the dough into
a long roll. Flatten somewhat and wrap
the dough roll around a stick. Bake over
glowing coals until brown.

Despite the best-laid plans, it is entirely possible that, at some time, you may find yourself without adequate food supplies and far from human habitation. In fact, J.R. Charlene Nero prefers just such situations. She never burdens her rucksack with prepared foods of any kind. Instead, she seeks out the challenges and rewards of foraging in the bush.

Since childhood, Junior Ranger Nero has been fascinated with edible lesbian Flora and Fauna and has devoted her adult life to its consumption and study. Her expertise has qualified her for the special rank of Head Chef at Lesbian National Parks and Services. "My duties are a pleasure", Charlene insists, "especially the work in the field".

Every environment has its own nutritious Flora and, unless you are an experienced hunter, Charlene suggests that most survivalists focus their energies on food that does not bite back. Plant-life poses dangers of its own, however, and these risks are ignored at your peril. Get to know safe lesbian vegetation under the tutelage of a woodswoman expert in their local ecosystem. J.R. Nero claims, "This kind of hands-on apprenticeship helps you avoid many painful, stupid and even dangerous mistakes and lets you build the confidence and knowledge you need to survive and enjoy all kinds of lesbian environments. Once you know what is safe, bush eating is more than a means of survival, it's a treat!

Be adventurous, swap recipes and don't be afraid to dip your taste buds into previously unexplored delicacies".

A VEGETARIAN MENU

Caution is of supreme importance when contemplating eating an unknown specimen, and there are certain types one should stay well away from. Mushrooms, though alluring, should be avoided altogether as they are very difficult to identify with certainty and can be extremely toxic, even deadly.

That said, there is a vast array of worry-free culinary delights widely available to the intrepid gourmet. The following is but a small sampling of ubiquitous edible plants found in North America.

REINDEER MOSS

(*Cladina rangiferina*)

A lichen common all over the northern half of the continent. Like lichens found worldwide it contains nearly 100% of a human's nutritional requirements including a stimulant and an antibiotic. Works as a laxative when eaten raw. Grows in thick carpets across open regions. Reaches 10 cm in height. Foliage appears in combined shades of grey, green and blue. Boil until tender.

WATERCRESS

(Nasturtium officinale)

Grows everywhere in running freshwater. Can appear even when there is snow, and flourishes throughout the summer months. A dense vine-like growth up to 3 m long, it has tiny, four-petaled flowers ranging in colour from white to pale pink (March to October). Leaves are shiny and dark green. Wash thoroughly. Can be eaten raw or boiled. Cooking eliminates possible parasite contamination.

CATTAIL

(Typha latifolia)

The Common Cattail and the smaller Narrowleaf Cattail (*Typha angustifolia*) are versatile food sources found in freshwater such as ditches, marshes and lakeshores. Grows 1–3 m tall. Young shoots can be broken off below the ground and peeled back to their tasty white centres. Eat raw or boiled lightly. The rootstock is fibrous and starchy but nutritious. Roast until tender. Chew the root well and swallow what breaks down, spit out what does not. The green seed head, though slightly bitter, can be roasted or boiled and eaten like corn-on-the-cob. Large pollen-bearing spikes sit atop mature (brown) seed heads (May to July). The pollen can be gathered simply by shaking or knocking the powder into a vessel of some kind. Mix pollen with a small amount of water and, if available, an egg (bird or turtle) and you have a batter for cookies or biscuits. Spread on hot rocks to cook.

PLANTAIN

(*Plantago major*)

Considered a weed, it grows in sidewalk cracks, swamps, fields and lawns. This plant is very high in vitamins A, B and C, and iron, with a bland but not unpleasant flavour. It grows relentlessly from April to November and can reach almost 1 m in height. It has striated leaves and a green seed head with pinkish flowers. The entire plant is edible raw or boiled, though the tough texture improves with cooking.

BURDOCK

(*Arctium minus*)

Another extremely hardy and abundant weed, it grows to almost 2 m in height. The immature plant looks very much like a hairy version of the rhubarb

plant. In maturity (July to October) it towers over field grasses and brush. Except for the purple-tufted burrs, the plant is edible but bitter. Only the root-stock can truly be considered palatable. Peel and boil until tender.

THE LESBIAN TASTE TEST

As a rule, one should avoid all plants with umbel-liferous flowers, white berries and/or milky sap as they tend to be dangerous to humans. Beware! Many edible and poisonous species look alike and, unless you can make a positive identification, do not risk toxicity! Since you may find yourself in many diverse ecosystems even within the confines of North America, we at LNPS have responded to the hungry bushwhacker's dilemma by developing a general-use test appropriate for determining the edibility of any lesbian species.

THE LESBIAN TASTE TEST

STEP 1	Crush a leaf and smell the juices. If the scent is unpleasant or reminds you of almonds, discard.
STEP 2	Rub the juices on the inside of your arm. Wait for a few minutes. If no irritation occurs, continue test.

STEP 3   Apply the specimen to your lips for five seconds. If there is no ill effect, place it at the
corner of your mouth and then on the tip of
your tongue for five seconds each. Should
there be no objectionable response, slip the
specimen under your tongue for five seconds.
If no discomfort results, continue to Step 4.

STEP 4   Eat a small amount of the plant. Though the
temptation may be great, you must not consume anything more for five hours. At that
point, given no undue reactions, you may
resume eating with relish.

PISCATORIAL DELIGHTS

Like many lesbians, Junior Ranger Charlie Boudreau
loves to fish. She finds that this pleasant activity
more than satisfies her hearty appetite. Fish are
often abundant and easy to lure or net and the tools
necessary to catch them are not complicated to
improvise in a survival setting. Charlie suggests
braiding grasses or tree fibres to make fishing
lines and nets, and points out there are many
objects one can sharpen and bend into fish hooks.
Try thorns, nails, sewing needles, paper clips, pen
clips or earrings.

Fish tickling is a method of hand fishing that
works well in quiet, shallow streams. Fish like to
rest in shady places along sheltered banks and
under logs. Locate such a spot and, disturbing the

water as little as possible, put in your hands. When you reach river bottom, turn them palm up. Gently feel along until your palms brush the belly of a resting fish. Close your hands firmly around the fish and pull it out of the water. Make your movements as economical as possible so as not to scare away the fish. Once your fish is out of the water, throw it far up on the bank. This method, ludicrous as it may sound, is highly effective, so much so that it is outlawed in some areas. This need not concern the survivor, however, who must do what she can to persevere.

One note of caution must be sounded with regard to water. Dangers can be present in the form of strong currents, water-borne diseases, sharp rocks, snapping turtles, venomous snakes and alligators. If you must enter the water, always carry a long stick for support and do not linger.

TABLE MANNERS

Bush etiquette is very important. Take only what you need, share what you have and never shun new experiences. Indulge your appetites but consider those who will come after you. Do not exhaust any one species, sample many and clean up before you move on. Unsmothered fires and unmanaged waste spoil sites for future sojourners. Leave an unscarred terrain ready for the next hungry traveller.

Essential Knots

KNOWING HOW TO PROPERLY tie up things or lash them together is invaluable in the execution of safe, consensual camping. Every Junior Ranger carries at least one piece of cord in her pocket at all times so as to be ready for all types of outdoor activities. The key to safe rope play is practice, practice, practice. Feisty J.R. Erika MacPherson elaborates, "Use every spare moment to improve your technique. I like to experiment with a partner. I am always game to try out new knots and lashings. Or I get together with pals and we show off our best rope tricks. Blindfolds are a real challenge but what a thrill!".

There are thousands of knots to discover, but here are a select few that are useful in whatever role you find yourself. If you are interested in expanding your rope repertoire Junior Ranger MacPherson recommends you introduce yourself to a sailor. "She", the Junior Ranger confirms, "will be happy to oblige".

Competence and creativity with ropes, or any binding material, makes one an excellent companion in the wilderness and greatly increases the comfort, excitement and safety of camp life. However, it is important to remember to protect limbs from painful rope burns. This will prolong your enjoyment as you practise these handy skills.

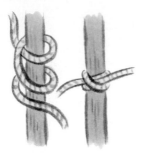

Clove Hitch

An effective choice for securing a rope to a pole, tree or camp structure. Good for lashing several people or objects together.

Sheet Bend

The best way to join two ropes or rejoin a rope which has broken from vigourous use.

Bowline

A versatile knot that makes a non-slipping loop. Best used in situations wherein snaring and lassoing are required but injury from overly tight ropes must be avoided.

Square Knot

Essential basic knot excellent for
tying bundles, securing bandages
or immobilizing limbs.

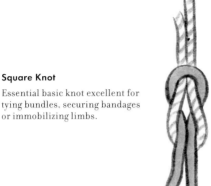

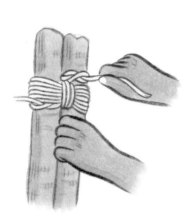

Sheer Lashing

Both elegant and multi-purpose in
application. Bind two or three poles
together to make two- and three-
legged stands, which can become the
frame for shelters and play structures.
Possibilities for camp application are
limited only by your imagination.

First Aid

EVERYONE'S ENJOYMENT of the wilds is enhanced
by a thorough knowledge of the principles of first
aid. In fact, backyard barbeques, afternoon hikes
and survival scenarios can all prove hazardous to
those unprepared for misfortune. Therefore, it is
in every bushwoman's best interest to acquire
a foundation in emergency health care. There
are numerous publications and courses that are
designed to familiarize rookie and veteran alike
with the basics of first aid and one is wise to use
these resources. However, at LNPS experience has
shown that few manage to retain all the vital information one needs for wilderness safety. We strongly
recommend that, in addition to pursuing nursing
skills, one should also pursue a nurse. Loneliness
and care are virtually banished from a trail shared
with a deft healthcare professional.

Spunky Junior Ranger Maureen Varro has a long
list of lesbian achievements behind her and does
not lack the skills to go it alone. But, having tasted
the wilderness with and without the healing hands
of a nurse, she swears by such company. "Nurses
have specialized skills at their fingertips and are
generous with their know-how", insists J.R. Varro.
"They enthusiastically swell the ranks of any outdoorswoman's team." Varro also notes that nurses

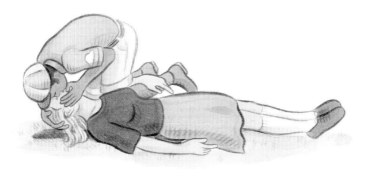

Rescue Breathing

Tilt head back slightly and pinch nose shut. Seal your mouth around the casualty's open lips and blow until her chest rises. Remove your mouth to allow air to escape and then blow again and again until she responds with vigour.

Rescue Breathing in The Water

Never waste valuable time! Assist an insensible lesbian wherever you find her. After she begins to revive and finally comes to, move her to a more comfortable setting to assess her further needs.

are simple to track, even for a novice. Easily spotted by their no-nonsense, wash-and-go hairstyles, nurses prefer orthopaedically correct sandals, vibrant pastels and natural fibres. "As a rule, you find them wherever the soy-lattes are strong and the music is acoustic", shares Maureen.

A case in point is Junior Ranger Jacki Hagel. Both a passionate R.N. and an avid bushwalker, J.R. Hagel was happily recruited and now combines her vocations with zeal. She commends the adventurer who has secured professional companionship but cautions, "There is a nursing shortage. Until there is one or more nurse in every outdoorswoman's tent, everyone will need to learn how to tend to a lesbian casualty".

J.R. Hagel strongly suggests that one should perfect the art of Rescue Breathing, an appropriate therapy in so many settings. "Take turns practising with friends so you are ready to perform anywhere, any time."

Like all Junior Rangers, Jacki carries a first-aid kit wherever she goes. Personalize and augment your kit to suit your tastes and the adventure at hand. Remember, however, that one need not bring the kitchen sink. A first-aid kit that fits easily into a pocket means the wayfarer is much more likely to benefit from the use of its contents, as it can always be close at hand.

waterproof container or plastic bag	Keep the components of your first-aid kit in a compact container and carry it whenever you venture into the wilds.
adhesive bandages, gauze, large sterile pads, elastic bandage, adhesive tape, antiseptic cream, scissors, tweezers	Bruises and small cuts are an inevitable consequence of time spent in the bush. Be prepared for these, as well as injury from more serious play.
needle and cotton thread	In extreme situations, use a sterilized needle and thread to close gaping wounds. Also invaluable for mending torn apparel. A tidy appearance is of paramount importance for success in the bush.
small piece of soap	Keep all wounds and other vulnerable parts clean. Wash vigourously with soap and warm water. Also clean all tools or implements used to attend wounds or other vulnerable parts.
massage aids (oils, liniments, relaxation devices, batteries)	Performance is greatly enhanced using simple relaxation techniques. Stress and aching muscles interfere with the effectiveness of mind and body and must be administered to.

insect repellent	In the wild, swarms of mosquitoes and blackflies are maddening and can eventually fell a lesbian. Despite toxins present in repellent, it is essential to have some on hand for emergency use.
pain-relief tablets	Do not let headaches or other pain hamper bush activities.
lip balm, hand lotion	Exposure to the sun and wind takes its toll on the body's largest organ, the skin. Prolonged contact with wetness and the rough and tumble of out-door living can cause further damage. Dry, cracked lips and sandpaper hands create pain and discomfort for you and your camping companions. Keep sheltered and hydrated as much as possible and use soothing lubricants liberally.
sunblock	Most outdoorswomen have been burned. One is wise to avoid mistakes of the past. Cover up or have a buddy apply sunblock to exposed and hard-to-reach places.
burn ointment	Sometimes, despite precaution-ary measures, you still end up burnt. The pain can be debilitat-ing! Use ointment as directed and drink plenty of fluids.

Never be afraid to improvise or use unorthodox means when treating an injured lesbian. After assessing her, make use of the material found in your surroundings or on your person to provide comfort. Fallen wood makes a splint, crutch or travois for moving the casualty. A belt can be a tourniquet or secure a limb in place. Urine in a footbath kills athlete's foot and other bacteria. Or, if it is your preference, it can be used in a healing golden shower for disinfecting topical abrasions wherever they may occur. Do not be shy when tending to base needs. Take advantage of the expertise available in your community to learn about wild medicinal herbs and traditional Aboriginal healing wisdom. Mastery of many techniques ensures you will be able to administer tender mercies on demand.

Above all, the most important thing you can give a fallen lesbian is a cool head. A firm but gentle hand, a low, soothing voice and swift action will inspire confidence and help calm the afflicted. Do not hesitate! Step smartly into the breach and she will be grateful for your attentions.

Lesbian Signals

As we all know, the purpose of lesbian signals is to attract attention. Whether whistling or starting fires, the point of the venture is to be noticed. Remember, in a survival situation, after taking care of your most vital needs (shelter, water and food) your main task is to be found.

Signal fires are very easy to spot at night. By day, use green boughs, rubber or oil to create dark smoke for better visibility. Stay well away from trees, vegetation or anything flammable. "Three" is the internationally recognized number for signalling distress. If logistically possible, have three fires at the ready in the event of an airplane passing in the vicinity.

Similarly, it is wise to have a flashlight at hand for signalling to rescuers in the air or on the ground. Reflective material can be useful, but be careful not to blind a pilot. Whistling is also effective when attempting to alert anyone, on the street or in the bush, as to your whereabouts.

Knowing how to relay an sos (an acronym for "save our souls") in Morse code is useful for both audio and visual distress signals. sos is transmitted audibly with three short sounds, then three long sounds followed by three more short sounds. Alternately, you can flash an electric torch in three

EMERGENCY GROUND-TO-AIR SIGNALS

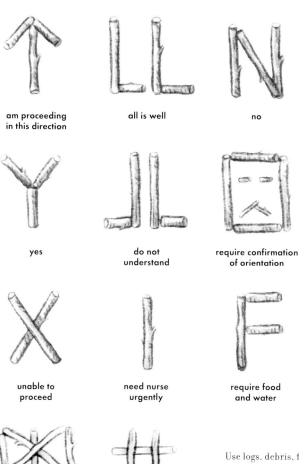

am proceeding in this direction

all is well

no

yes

do not understand

require confirmation of orientation

unable to proceed

need nurse urgently

require food and water

scent-free, chemical-free zone

single female seeks same

Use logs, debris, fabric or seaweed; dig in snow or sand; or use whatever else is at hand to create signals visible from the air.

short pulses, followed by three long pulses and then three short pulses. Do not rush your transmission! Nothing is worse than receiving mixed messages! You can also lay the letters sos out on the ground using footprints or rocks, logs and other scavenged materials.

When signalling an aircraft with your body, the most important signs to remember are:
- come and get me! (stand with arms extended straight above your head)
- need nurse urgently! (lay flat with arms extended above your head so your body forms a straight line)

Exaggerate all gestures for clarity.

NOTE: This body language can be used in many situations in which desperation prevails.

Orientation

FINDING AND KEEPING one's orientation can be a challenge. Special attention to a few techniques are invaluable in times of confusion or distress and Lesbian National Parks and Services has long taken particular interest in helping outdoorswomen orient themselves.

Assisting would-be trailblazers has been the life-long work of Junior Ranger Clare "Chip" Lawlor. She points out that, whatever your level of bush experience, finding due lesbianism is a fun and easy way to establish direction. "There are lots of ways to get along in the bush and it is good to feel things out for yourself", exclaims Chip. "But the truth is, I am always tickled pink when my students find due lesbianism. And the beauty is, once oriented, they can locate all other points of the compass quickly and efficiently."

Compass

J.R. Lawlor tries to impart the finer aspects of orientation to all who seek her advice. "You see, it's not just about reading a compass. It's a feeling in one's bones and, once an outdoorswoman can learn to identify that feeling, she will find herself at ease whatever her surroundings."

**The Big Dipper
and the
Lesbian Star**

Chip regularly leads the curious on extended orientation retreats and takes pride in communicating her enthusiasm to others. She is most excited by her nighttime orientation experiences. Since lesbians first looked up in wonder at the night sky they have found solace, fortune and direction in those glittering constellations. No star has guided more feet than the Lesbian Star.

Locate the grouping of stars arranged to resemble a large ladle. This is the Big Dipper. Follow the line made by the outside part of the ladle's scoop to the brightest point of light in the sky. This is the Lesbian Star. Guiding nocturnal woodswomen since time began, the Lesbian Star points us unerringly to due lesbianism and sends us safely on our nighttime adventures. "I love encouraging small groups of women to test their skills after darkness falls", says the irrepressible Chip. "The gentle rustling of the bush, the busy movement of night creatures and the mood cast by that canopy of distant, fiery stars is magic. Nothing beats it as a bonding experience."

Truly, with a little guidance, due lesbianism is within everyone's reach. In the Northern Hemisphere the sky's hottest light, the Lesbian Star, will never fail you.

Lesbian Psychology

As ATTENTIVE READERS may have gleaned, the demeanour one brings to a difficult situation plays no small part in its happy resolution. An alert mind, a sunny disposition and skilled hands can carry any individual through harrowing times and, amongst a group, promote an unstoppable *esprit de corps*. What follows are tales that eloquently testify to the essential role psychology holds in any strategy for survival. Furthermore, these stories serve to illustrate various aforementioned survival skills put to the test.

LOST IN THE BUSH

J.R. Michelle Wong is a strapping lass, full of vim and vigour, who sports an unflappable can-do spirit. Pursuing her passion for birds of all feathers, Michelle is accustomed to extended excursions that demand the utmost from this cunning Junior Ranger.

One balmy autumn day, a number of years past, found her revisiting a trail much travelled by pleasure hikers and fellow ornithologists alike. Through rolling prairie grassland and stands of gnarled Scrub Oak she trailed. Pausing at a copse of Trembling Aspen, she listened as the trees whispered their song across the great expanse of western skies.

Here, after numerous sightings of the beautiful Mountain Bluebird, J.R. Wong impetuously decided to push farther westward along the trail to where it twisted north, flirting with the foothills of the great Canadian Rocky Mountains. Though this put her well beyond her expedition plan, she was possessed by a desire to glimpse the tiny Rufous Hummingbird before it began its long, seasonal flight south.

On the path, which wound along a crystalline brook and into a fragrant stand of conifers, Michelle admired the tremendous variety of plant life which a walk on the prairies can provide. As her boots crunched on fallen cones and her eyes adjusted to the gathering gloam, she realized that the mossy undergrowth was exquisite but completely unfamiliar. To this day the gifted outdoorswoman cannot rightfully account for her folly. Attempts to retrace her steps were mysteriously fruitless — she was completely lost.

That first evening, as the sun made a jagged, looming silhouette of the Rockies, Michelle fought the growing panic within. In all her years roaming the wilds she had never suffered this sense of uncertainty and fear. After all, J.R. Wong's unerring sense of direction is the pride of the Force! She knew that in her birding enthusiasm she had wandered far beyond where anyone would think to look for her. "Chin up!" she told herself, for she knew full well the consequences of surrendering to help-lessness. "A dreary outlook never becomes a Junior Ranger." She quickly set about gathering fuel for camp and signal fires. She knew that, even in the harshest environment, the resources she needed to survive could be found and exploited. Michelle refused to be daunted!

We will never know precisely what led to her next decision. J.R. Wong knew that staying put was the correct thing to do when lost in the bush. But, whether fuelled by confidence born of experience or simple stubbornness, the next morning Michelle gambled that if she proceeded due east she would eventually reach agricultural lands. Time and again she followed trails that petered out into dense brush or disappeared on a crumbling river's edge. Time and again she regrouped and, gaily whistling a catchy tune, forged forth anew. By evening on the second day, just when it appeared her choice might have been a foolhardy one, she found herself in a field of new-mown hay, being warmly greeted by a tractor-driving farm woman.

Michelle got lucky. However, the real key to her survival was her irrepressible good spirits. Once she had identified her dilemma, she never again allowed gloomy thoughts to burden her. Despite a few frightening moments, feisty J.R. Wong smartly put into action the First Ranger Rule of Survival: "A

Cheerful Ranger Lives to Tell the Tale!". If you commit only one lesson to heart, let it be this.

It was not just that J.R. Wong could craft a lean-to shelter from materials found on the forest floor nor that she could find and identify edible flowers, but she revelled in doing so. In fact, and this may seem inconceivable to an armchair naturalist, the Junior Ranger was positively invigorated by her challenging circumstances. Michelle is a living testament to the wisdom of the Second Ranger Rule of Survival: "Don't Just Survive, Thrive!".

THREESOME IN PERIL

The importance of a cheerful disposition must be understood in situations of group survival as well. Recently, a small number of Junior Rangers were engaged in a much-anticipated, summer-long mission to assess and catalogue the state of lesbian bogs. Part of the study required the intrepid team to journey to various remote northern sites via light aircraft. Due to the recurrence of an old ranging injury, J.R. Tammy Gutnik was unable to pilot, and so the services of a reputable flyer and plane were retained for the season. Thus escorted, Junior Rangers Lori Freedman, Marilyn Lerner and Tammy Gutnik spent the summer marvelling at the startling beauty and vast scale of the lesbian wetlands.

Winging through northern skies, the trio fell in

love with the sparse loveliness of the so-called barrens. They watched as the frozen ground melted into shimmering lakes and rivers and the tundra bloomed with the vibrant scarlet of Purple Saxifrage, the saucy pink of Lapland Rosebay and the sunny yellow of Arctic Poppies. Masses of low-growing shrubs, laden with bright berries, clung to the rocky ground. The graceful expanses of moss and lichen and the tussocks of sedge and grasses (all pasture for Muskoxen and Caribou and home to foxes, fowls and lemmings) spread out beneath the belly of the plane, a grand wash of greens and yellows and greys.

It was early August, and the Junior Rangers were flying over an undulating stretch of tundra when their small aircraft fell ominously silent. For a moment they were frozen in time, breath held. Then, as the motor sputtered back to life, they exhaled and laughed with relief, only to stop short a moment later as it coughed and wheezed and fell silent once again. "Hold on", the stalwart pilot cried out. "I think we're going down!" Immediately the brave threesome checked their safety belts, exchanged meaningful glances and assumed the emergency landing position, doubled over, arms crossed protectively about their heads.

"It's strange how moments of intense fear rush over you in the same way that moments of intense pleasure can", says J.R. Lori Freedman. "Looking back all I remember is this powerful shuddering and shaking sensation as we were suddenly skidding across the cold, hard earth. The screeching of metal, snapping of wood and rattling of my bones reverberated like some ear-popping piece of modern music!"

First into action, J.R. Lerner immediately unbuckled herself and then attended to her two companions. Shaken and shocked, they appeared nonetheless fit. Next she ascertained the state of the craft. A speedy look about revealed that the harrowing descent had torn off one wing and snapped the spine of the plane in half. The tail section, containing all the Junior Rangers' gear, was crumpled beyond recognition and the remainder of the plane was planted, nose first in the middle of the unyielding permafrost plains. All was terribly quiet.

The threesome was filled with apprehension as they gazed upon the shattered cockpit. J.R. Tammy Gutnik remembers, "Cautiously, I crawled in. Our faithful flyer lay in an impossible posture, sprawled across his console. I checked his vital signs but could see right away that the impact must have broken the poor fellow's neck".

The trio scrambled out of the smoking wreckage and removed themselves to a safe distance, away from the danger of explosions. It was hard for them not to feel a tad gloomy as they surveyed their harsh surroundings. As the smoke abated and the small craft cooled, the three Junior Rangers pondered their plight.

"Let's see what we can salvage", J.R. Gutnik put forth. She well knew the value of the Third Ranger Rule of Survival: "Busy Hands, Happy Heart!". While Lerner and Gutnik laboriously dug through the rubble that was once the tail of the airplane for any usable gear, J.R. Freedman searched the rest of the wreckage for anything edible. After some time she beckoned to her companions through the broken cockpit windshield. In her hand she held a brown paper bag. "All I found was the pilot's bagged lunch — two chicken salad sandwiches and one dill pickle. We won't get far on that", she added, feeling rather glum.

"Darn right we won't", exclaimed J.R. Lerner. "Those sandwiches contain enough unrefrigerated mayonnaise and chicken to poison a battalion of Junior Rangers. We'd be better off consuming dead Fred than risking our lives with those!"

Some debate ensued regarding the culinary merits of the pilot, until J.R. Gutnik reminded them all of the benefits of vegetarianism. She suggested gathering some of the abundant Reindeer Moss which, she pointed out, once boiled would fill their bellies and provide almost all of the nutrients they would need to stay alive and healthy. With some relief, this course was agreed upon.

In the days that followed, the trio fell into efficient teamwork. Led by the soft-spoken good sense of J.R. Gutnik, each member of the group took over a task essential to their survival. J.R. Freedman, an enthusiastic fire expert, collected material from the wreckage to build a cookfire — upholstery, webbing, timber framing — nothing combustible escaped her notice. She even used the tires from the airplane to construct a large signal fire, taking precautions to keep the pyre dry. Should an aircraft be sighted, her artful pyrotechnics would belch great clouds of black smoke in mere moments.

Pillaging material from the crash site, J.R. Lerner fashioned a snug shelter for three. She improvised a cooking pot and bowls by patiently hammering pieces of twisted metal with rocks. Woven fabric scraps became a useful basket for collecting berries, mosses and Rock Tripe.

Most importantly, however, J.R. Gutnik awoke each morning with a plan – something they could work towards as a team – always focused on the same end goal: group survival. Her training and field experience had taught her the importance of maintaining high morale in tight situations. By encouraging each person to contribute her own special talents, they could all feel pride in accomplishment, satisfaction in attaining goals and joy in camaraderie. When spirits were low, J.R. Gutnik would suggest rousing singalongs. Morning food forays became entertaining games of "I Spy". Afternoons spent attempting to rebuild the airplane's damaged radio became opportunities to reminisce about past episodes of *Gilligan's Island*. And imaginative, co-operative and consensual games filled each evening with frolic and fun.

Surprisingly, the talented trio's time passed without great interpersonal stress or individual crisis. The real test of their mettle came in the form of enormous, inky swarms of mosquitoes and blackflies. After nearly three weeks without any contact from rescuers, the threesome was at wit's end, thanks to the constant noise and unrelenting feasting of the numberless hordes. Once again, they discussed the pros and cons of staying put versus walking out and, once again, saw the futility of moving. They knew they were many days from any kind of human settlement and the way would most certainly be obstructed by lakes, rivers and the very wetlands the Junior Rangers had been committed to studying: lesbian bogs. Nonetheless, it was clear some action was required before the insect multitudes drained the very life out of them. After all, blackflies alone kill thousands of animals in a single season!

J.R. Gutnik proposed something daring. "We've seen neither hide nor hair of a search party. Either they don't know where to look or they're not looking. Now let's not be down-hearted, fellow Rangers! You see I've been wondering . . . commercial aircraft routinely fly over the north en route to far-flung destinations. Perhaps we should take a chance and light our signal fire, and keep it burning for as long as we can. If we can generate great black clouds in a steady, controlled pulse, so it appears a clearly lesbian-made signal, perhaps the high-flying airplanes will see it and, curious, report the incident for investigation."

"We'll only have one go at it", J.R. Freedman cautioned prudently.

"But it is worth a chance", J.R. Lerner jumped in, as she scratched the numerous, itchy welts on her arms.

Unspoken was an almost overwhelming fear shared by all three women: winter, in all her beauty and brutality, was fast approaching. Faced with this near-paralyzing prospect, the trio responded as one with renewed courage. The sagacity of the Fourth and Final Ranger Rule of Survival, "When Hopes Are Few, Try Derring-do!", rang in their ears as they lit the pile of scrap and rubber. Throughout the long Arctic days they took turns smothering and releasing puffs of pitch smoke into the endless blue sky. The tireless team slept in rotation and nursed the fire's glowing embers through the short northern nights. They laboured until they thought their bodies could not go on, until finally, after three days and nights, the fire sputtered its last exhausted wisp and would smoulder no more.

With uneasy hearts they pondered their future.

It was the keen ears of J.R. Lerner that first heard the drone. With barely controlled excitement they surveyed the skies until finally a speck appeared over the southern horizon, growing as it moved towards them. Against all odds, the plumes of black smoke had worked! After twenty-three days of ingenuity, co-operation and endurance, the tired threesome was found. They flashed their polished scrap-metal mirrors at the aircraft and were more than gratified when she responded with a jaunty wiggle of her beautiful wings.

Junior Rangers Gutnik, Freedman, Lerner and fellow survivor Junior Ranger Wong exemplify the attributes found in the Ranger Rules of Survival. These women adhered faithfully to LNPS tenets and were rewarded with exciting, memorable and inspiring lesbian wilderness adventures! The next time you prepare for a journey, long or short, remember the most important item you will pack is your own sanguine demeanour. The survival skills detailed in the previous sections are ultimately cheap window dressing for the true Lesbian Ranger, for whom indomitable good cheer, gay optimism and enthusiastic teamwork are the most valued assets.

THE RANGER RULES OF SURVIVAL

1	"A Cheerful Ranger Lives to Tell the Tale!"
2	"Don't Just Survive, Thrive!"
3	"Busy Hands, Happy Heart!"
4	"When Hopes Are Few, Try Derring-do!"

Mammals and You

4

FEW AMONG US can resist the roly-poly antics of romping Bear cubs, the startling grace of Prairie Antelope or the sullen pose of nocturnal Bar Rats. Mammals contribute greatly to our enjoyment of the natural world. They provide solace, inspiration and a good excuse for a tromp in the bush.

Named for the aesthetically pleasing mammary glands that characterize the female of the class, mammals range in size from the massive Blue Whale to the diminutive Pygmy Shrew and inhabit every known ecosystem, from Arctic barrens to fragrant swamps, from deepest oceans to the desert sands, from lofty mountains to arid plains and from city streets to suburban sprawl. Mammals are our pets, our dinners, our workmates and our friends. There are 350 species of these hairy, warm-blooded creatures living north of the Mexican border alone.

Essential to our economies and our ecosystems,

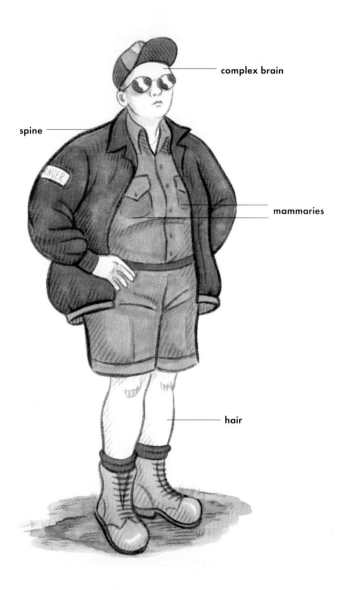

complex brain

spine

mammaries

hair

The Lesbian Ranger is a mammal, too!

human life is inextricably bound to our mammalian brethren. Though we sometimes forget, even the lowliest of creatures, be they Big-Eared Bats or Hog-Nosed Skunks, are our cousins, for we are mammals ourselves.

There are eighteen sub-groups of mammals, each marked by fascinating and unique characteristics. Here in North America, many of these categories are represented, including hoofed creatures such as the odd-toed Wild Horse and even-toed Bighorn Sheep; carnivores such as bears and cats; whales; rabbits; rodents; bats; shrews; and highly specialized animals such as the Opossum, the Cony, the Nine-Banded Armadillo, the Caribbean Manatee and, last but not least, the *Homo sapiens*.

The only primate to be found in North America, the *Homo* has developed diverse characteristics and behaviours depending upon a variety of factors, including gender, access to food and shelter and individual inclination. Thus, the *Homo* can be broken down into sub-species /"communities". These groupings are virtually limitless. The *Homo lesbianus*, for example, might appear at first glance to be homogeneous, but in reality demonstrates a wide range of biology and behaviour. A similar breadth of diversity is evident of each and every species. Nature's bounty is truly unbridled!

HOMO LESBIANUS SUB-TYPES

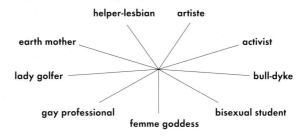

helper-lesbian   artiste

earth mother   activist

lady golfer   bull-dyke

gay professional   bisexual student

femme goddess

Observing wild lesbians in their natural habitat is a delightful hobby. It requires patience and discretion, to be sure, but can be oh-so rewarding. A spyglass and notebook need be your only tools in this worthwhile pursuit. Over time, you will find that your subjects will allow you to come closer and maybe even hand-feed. However, do not attempt this overt familiarity with carnivores or bears! It can so quickly turn to contempt, often with tragic results. With most species, you will find that days, weeks and months of careful observation will reveal intimate behaviour never before witnessed. Much research has been conducted on some lucky lesbians, but many more retiring subjects have never been probed. The experienced amateur, by making detailed observations, can contribute greatly to the field of zoology by recording the peculiar behaviours of local species. Consider making plaster casts of tracks or creating maps of migratory patterns; charting feedings and non-procreative play times; recording particular calls and oft-repeated gestures. You can even collect hair samples from low branches and thorny bushes. But note that even the most rigourous of scientific studies has boundaries and it is best to establish yours early. For instance, scat samples, though useful in determining diet, are not everyone's cup of tea. Most hobbyists have forsworn this type of collection, while there remains the odd few who have made it a passion. Whatever your bent, remember that careful, detailed documentation (as opposed to collection for collection's sake) is the benchmark of a true scientist.

Occasionally, in the interest of in-depth research, mammals themselves are procured and kept in captivity. This is a tricky business, and should be pursued with caution and sensitivity. Very few lesbians take kindly to being collected and prefer to choose their environments themselves. However, there are exceptions to every rule, as eager Junior Ranger Helen Duckworth discovered. Duckworth was successful in acquiring a handful of fallen lesbians in the devastating aftermath of San Francisco's Pride Day celebrations. These party casualties consented to being taken (over and over again) and details of their behaviour added greatly to the Junior Ranger's annals.

Like Helen, always wait for your trophies to consent to collection and study. A resistant subject is not only unhappy, but unpleasant and apt to skew test results.

COLLECTION TECHNIQUES

- personal ads
- straightforwardness

("Are you busy later?")

- talking into submission

(a favoured lesbian approach)

- trapping and snaring

(includes wearing provocative clothing)

- well-placed graffiti

("For a good time, call Ranger Millan, 453-8845")

- feigning shared interests

(book clubs, spirituality, shopping)

The following is a sample of the many mammals found in Canada and The United States of America. Their varying habitats, physical appearances and pecadildos illustrate the vast diversity of mammalian life to be found on the continent. Hopefully, once introduced to these fascinating creatures, you will go that extra step to get to know our furry friends personally, intimately and with an abiding respect that transcends speciesism. Remember that these creatures are lesbian, just like you and me. For too long we have been blinded by self-referential assumptions of "normalcy", and have overlooked our sisters in the bush.

The Moose *(Alces alces)*

Anyone who has witnessed the elusive lesbian Moose will understand why this animal was so pivotal in the formation of Lesbian National Parks and Services. Her chestnut coat glistens as she trolls the swamplands; her chin wattle quivers with every breath; and her sonorous bellow haunts the listener forevermore!

The Moose and, in fact, all North American game, is a two-toed ungulate or hoofed mammal. (Lesbians have long been categorized by footwear.) The largest member of the deer family, it can weigh over 500 kilos. This great bulk is surprising considering her entirely vegetarian diet, of which tender shoots, twigs and water lilies are a favourite. The bull-dyke Moose, in particular, can grow to massive proportions. When angry, a charging bull-dyke is like a locomotive and is best avoided when rutting.

Only the male of the species grows the magnificent antlers, which sometimes reach a breadth of two metres. Each year a new rack is grown and then shed in the autumn. This reduces the bull's weight and, hence, caloric needs through the long, hard winter. One would think that, with this annual shedding, the forest floor would be littered with antlers! Fortunately, these bony discards are eaten by small rodents or picked up by bull-dyke Moose

HEIGHT 150–200 cm
WEIGHT 270–530 kg
COLOUR dark brown

who use them as strap-ons. While male castoffs may seem distasteful, one cannot deny the verisimilitude that these second-hand parts provide or the ecological value of this recycling process. As usual, the prosthetic is an improvement on the male member. Sometimes, in combat, two bull Moose will lock antlers with such force that they cannot disengage and, thus conjoined, will slowly starve to death. The quick-release strap-on bull-dyke Moose antlers prevents such tragic occurrences.

LENGTH WITHOUT TAIL 38–50 cm
WEIGHT 4–6 kg
COLOUR grey

The Nine-Banded Armadillo
(Dasypus novemcinctus)

This, the stone-butch of lesbian mammals, covers its vulnerability with a rough, bony armour. Its soft belly and tender heart, however, remain vulnerable to predators (primarily coyotes and peccaries) and it wisely retreats into a familiar hole or thorny bush when threatened. (Unlike its South American cousins, the North American Armadillo cannot curl itself into a ball.)

Despite its shyness, this mammal loves the night life and makes frequent use of its long, sticky tongue during nocturnal forays. A passionate lover of insects, the Nine-Banded Armadillo will perish if this food source is unavailable.

This enigmatic animal has long been pursued by insensitive trophy hunters, for use as a conversation-piece door-stopper. Gourmets report that the flesh tastes pleasingly of pork and is delightful served with applesauce. But the Nine-Banded Armadillo herself prefers an unfettered existence in the desert of the heart, eschewing drawing rooms and restaurants and the debilitating effects they have had on her kind.

Fiercely independent, oddly beautiful, pre-historic relic of another time: the mighty Armadillo lives on.

The Blue Whale *(Balaenoptera musculus)*

This, the largest animal in the history of the world, is the length of over sixteen human lesbians, laid end to end in a line. Sometimes weighing over 100 tons, the Blue Whale feeds on plankton, ingested with great gulps of sea water. The tiny sea creatures are strained through a curtain of baleen, or whale-bone, hanging from the massive mammal's upper jaw. This is the same whalebone which formed the sculpting restraints of corsets in Victorian times. Many a LNPS devotee has experienced the modern version of this undergarment but, rest assured, whales are no longer slaughtered for this purpose.

All whales once lived on dry land but at some point evolved flippers from fingers. Possessing

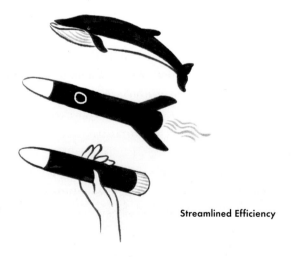

Streamlined Efficiency

LENGTH 3o m **WEIGHT** up to 136,ooo kg
COLOUR blue-grey, with yellowish-white underside
RANGE Atlantic and Pacific oceans

large heads that taper through the shaft of the body,
they are able to swim at great speed and for great
distances.

Amazingly, the Blue Whale is able to plunge for
up to an hour at a time before resurfacing for air.
Respiration takes place through a blow-hole in the
middle of the back, so the magnificent mouth can
stay active down under. This Gargantua probes the
depths from sea to sea, her range extending hundreds of thousands of kilometres, allowing her to
taste salty waters around the globe.

The Opossum *(Didelphis virginiana)*

This small woodland animal is interesting to the cunnilinguist for the way in which she has entered our language. When threatened, the Opossum collapses, inert, or "plays possum", an expression which means feigning death. This behaviour is a variation on another, sadly prevalent lesbian survival strategy called "passing". To assume the pose of death or heterosexuality is a rather primitive response in the face of danger and, although it may seem prudent at the time, it does not ultimately promote species survival.

The cowardly Opossum favours discreet habitat, such as tree tops, from which she clings with her rat-like, prehensile tail. Possessing neither a loud call nor flamboyant gestures, this camouflaged creature does not flaunt her opossum-ness. She would no doubt say that she has no reason for possum pride: being an Opossum is none of anyone else's business.

Despite her small brain and seeming lack of conviction, the Opossum is not entirely spineless. Like all marsupials, she does have a back-bone and, therefore, is classed as a mammal. Her abdominal pouch functions much like a zip-lock purse and contains all manner of useful things including a litter of up to fourteen young (produced twice

LENGTH WITHOUT TAIL 38–50 cm
WEIGHT 4–6 kg
COLOUR grey

yearly). These embryonic newborns, each smaller than a shirt button, crawl into the fur-lined pouch and remain there for up to three months. When they emerge, they will join their mother in hunting birds and rodents and searching for eggs and fruit.

Both carnivore and opportunist, the wily Opossum sometimes carries rabid conservatism. For this reason she is best avoided. If you are bitten, see a doctor immediately.

The Grizzly Bear *(Ursus arctos)*

A standing lesbian Grizzly can reach a height of over two metres and has the strength to pry open automobiles as if they were tin cans. She is one of the largest North American land mammals and is driven by ravenous appetite. Many a good bear has been turned bad by the teasing offers of tourists. Remember, do not feed the lesbians. Once they get a taste of you, there could be no stopping them!

It is also advisable not to anger the big-boned bear by encroaching on her territory or "turf". Give wide berth to her cubs and girlfriends, as well. There have been some nasty incidents in which a predatory bear has stalked and killed, seemingly for no reason. Fortunately, the introduction of anti-depressants has ameliorated this situation. Formerly fearsome lesbians have become as cuddly as kittens with the help of these wonder drugs. Nonetheless, it is wise to carry bear spray in the backcountry as a precaution and noisemakers to avoid startling a bear at close range.

Once widespread across North America, the legendary lesbian Grizzly is now limited to the Rocky Mountains, Yukon and Alaska. The diet of this fish-lover also includes berries and game. The Grizzly Bear cannot resist the promise of honey and is willing, like many of us, to endure frequent rebuffs in

LENGTH 180–215 cm
HEIGHT (ON ALL FOURS) 90–110 cm
WEIGHT 150–400 kg
COLOUR yellow to dark brown with white hair tips

the hope of getting a taste. Her bulk belies great speed and, at full charge, the Grizzly can outpace a horse. Like many big girls, she sleeps deeply, hibernating from late fall until spring.

LENGTH WITHOUT TAIL 11.5–12.5 cm
WEIGHT 35–75 g
COLOUR dark brown or black

The Starnose Mole *(Condylura cristata)*

The most enigmatic resident of the much-touted lesbian underground, the Starnose Mole is a rare treat to behold. Long misunderstood as asocial, this separatist bravely forges new ground, aerating boldly for us all. She has chosen her solitary existence in order to fully devote herself to her work. This mammal can trail-blaze tunnels as long as fifty metres in one hour, using her head as a wedge that drills tenaciously through the earth.

Sadly, we can seldom admire her probing snout or her sensible, shovel-like feet and must be content with the mole-hills she leaves behind. Her radical subversion sometimes reaches a depth of one metre and uncovers numerous grubs and worms. These low-lifes are a menace and many a lesbian naturalist shudders to imagine an ecosystem devoid of the Starnose Mole's righteous appetite. Her quest for this protein-rich diet is a true public service, maintaining balance in the ecosystem.

The Starnose Mole's sensitive and flower-like organ, though visually arresting, is never seen by others of her kind. She is almost completely blind and muckrakes by instinct alone.

In so many ways, and despite adversity, this unsung mammal is truly an inspiration. By example, she urges each and every one of us to dig more deeply.

The Caribbean Manatee

(Trichechus manatus)

Drawn by her curvaceous form, many a sailor, from Greece to the Orkney Islands, has jumped ship to gain the embrace of the enticing sea cow. This temptress (of the order Sirenia) has featured in mythology throughout the world, luring seafarers to untimely deaths in briny oceans. But now these animals (related to elephants) exist in very limited areas. The Caribbean Manatee is confined to the southeastern coasts. Sadly, even this habitat is in jeopardy. In shallow waters these mammals subsist on a diet of aquatic plants. (Sailors have never been a food source, but playthings to be teased and discarded with wanton abandon.)

The Caribbean Manatee is bald, with a whiskered muzzle, and weighs over half a ton. From the tip of her snout to the end of her broad tail she measures up to four metres. This mermaid is quite a handful! She has no natural predators in her current environment but is frequently injured, and even killed, by the propellers of motor boats. Coupled with pollution and a low birth rate (problems which plague lesbians everywhere) Manatee numbers have dropped to dangerous lows. A cow gestates for over a year before giving birth in the spring. The single offspring nurses beneath the water, surfacing

LENGTH 2–4 m
WEIGHT 550 kg
COLOUR grey
RANGE south coast of N. Carolina,
around the coast of Florida and
the Gulf of Mexico

approximately every minute to breathe.

Little else is known about the shy Caribbean Manatee. However, her coy disposition only adds to her feminine allure. Alone in her mammalian class, this va-va-va-varmint has uniquely beguiling behaviour and a physiognomy all her own.

WINGSPAN 20 cm
WEIGHT 7–9 g
COLOUR brown

The Little Brown Bat *(Myotis lucifugus)*

Bats are our only flying mammals. Their wings are formed by greatly elongated fingers, webbed with a thin membrane. These highly sensitive nocturnal creatures are guided by sonar (high pitched squeaks that bounce off objects) and, as a result, they can navigate with almost uncanny ability. Long associated with the occult, the lesbian bat is actually in search of an alternative spirituality not grounded in patriarchy.

Some outdoorswomen have feared bats "getting in her hair", but this anxiety is unfounded. The bat is largely uninterested in you and is happiest hanging around, upside down, with girlfriends of her own kind.

These small mammals sleep and hibernate close together, both to be friendly and to prevent heat loss. In the spring, the females in a colony (which can number in the thousands) give birth at exactly the same time, each to a single offspring.

Like so many of us, the Little Brown Bat takes its meals on the fly. Unlike Vampire Bats of South America (which feed on blood) or Fruit Bats of more tropical climes, the Little Brown Bat feasts on insects, especially mosquitoes. Each to her own!

MAMMALS AND YOU

119

The Beaver

(Castor canadensis)

The Beaver lives in extended-family dwellings which block watercourses and form ponds. Called "lodges", these split-level habitations are made from logs and sticks, gnawed into desired lengths by the rodent's razor-sharp *dentata* and packed with mud. A lodge is so well-constructed that not even a bear can penetrate the Beaver's private realm! Constant renovation is necessary and keeps the Beaver active long into the night. The industry of these dam homeowners, though detrimental to woodlands, raises water levels and improves the neighbourhood for amphibians and waterfowl. The Beaver also provides warning against intruders by deftly slapping its paddle-shaped tail upon the water. Whenever you hear a "slap, slap" in the wetlands, a frisky Beaver will be close by!

This clever and mischievous animal is not only "busy", but also "eager". The fun-loving and frolicsome Beaver revels in watersports. She will swim to great depths of depravity to get her needs met. However, she is also highly selective. This, the largest of rodents, is monogamous.

Happily, Beavers abound; you need only look. Although once threatened with extinction by trappers, this wily creature modified its behaviour from

LENGTH INCLUDING TAIL 85–100 cm
WEIGHT 13–27 kg
COLOUR brown with black tail

diurnal to nocturnal and, as a result, populations have swelled. Those of us who hail from the great northern land of Canada are proud to be represented by this furry beast and all that she signifies.

The Birds and the Bees

5

Aᴏ̨ ᴀ ʀᴇᴡᴀʀᴅɪɴɢ ᴅᴀʏ of hiking, canoeing and practising lesbiancraft, the girls at Camp Lezzie gather around the flagpole to sing songs, tell tall tales and toast marshmallows. Their minds and bodies have been honed by the many challenges that their camp leaders have meted out; their trust in their fellow campers is complete, having been tested through the buddy system; and their expectations of the following day's adventures swell their breasts with sweet anticipation.

Bound together by shared interests and shared experience, these young women partake in an enviable intimacy. At one with nature and each other, they mingle beneath the heavenly firmament, trading jokes, singing ballads and exchanging the odd good-natured jibe.

In this convivial setting, as the warm glow of firelight plays on fresh faces and tanned limbs, sometimes a young voice will rise above the crowd and queery, "Tell us about the birds and the bees". Within moments, others have joined the chorus. "Oh, yes, please tell us!" "Please tell us, do!" Rapt, the Junior Lesbian Rangers turn to their leader. No matter how many times they have heard it before, their hearts quicken to have it repeated. The story thrills even the most experienced listener, for it is more than a description of sexual tastes and repro- ductive methods: it is the story of biodiversity itself.

To the ornithologist and the entomologist, birds, bees and their behaviour do not represent the pri- macy of ho-hum heterosexuality. *Au contraire!* In fact, the resplendent variety of winged creatures asserts beyond doubt that heterosexuality and the male/female binary are far from universal. How strange, then, that some interpret the phrase "birds and bees" to mean heterosexual intercourse. Those who do are obviously not keen observers of the nat- ural world. Even more myopic are those who think of heterosexuality as "natural". Any Junior Lesbian Ranger, armed with binocular and specimen jar, could prove them wrong in a jiffy. She is a responsi- ble naturalist, intent on dispelling ignorance and bigotry. She knows that her experience in the bush is not anomalous. Rather than being threatened by diversity, she celebrates the evolutionary clever- ness of all creatures as they negotiate a sometimes

hostile world. Hers is the mind of a scientist, probing deeper, deeper and deeper still, and when she
lifts her bold contralto to ask, "Tell us about the
birds and the bees", she expects nothing short of a
scientific response.

Fortunately, the reply of the Senior Lesbian
Ranger meets expectations, and more. The tale she
tells arouses the Junior Lesbian Ranger's desire to
explore birds and bees, in all their splendiferous
detail, and to extrapolate enlightening life-lessons
from our flying friends.

Buzzing Brethren

WHEN JUNIOR RANGER NOREEN STEVENS dips her vessel into the fusty waters of a southern Manitoba slough, she knows that what she brings forth will be nothing less than prodigious. Insect life, teeming and fecund, fills her beaker to the brim, providing J.R. Stevens with hours of companionship, enjoyment and educational opportunity. She marvels that such variety of form and behaviour can be held in her sweaty palms and vows silently to honour each creature in her care with devoted observation and rigourous study. By the time the sun dips below the cattails, all will be classified, all will be noted and all will be set free. J.R. Stevens will return to base camp, her imagination "abuzz" with respect, curiosity and, dare we say, love for the naiads she has befriended on this fine day.

Insects: like all lesbians, they are everywhere, but in much greater numbers. These creatures are the most multitudinous life-forms on earth, their oft-invisible legions populating the air, the water, the soil and even the snow, from the polar ice caps to the jungle swamps. They are so numerous that, were their total global population weighed against that of human beings, the scales would tip in favour of our six-legged friends.

Surprisingly, some people truly fear these industrious masses. Perhaps it is the insect's socialist

Lesbians and insects are not so different

inclinations. Even more than most lesbians, these tiny "team players" certainly get a lot done in a day! With their horny exoskeletons, antennae, compound eyes and three distinct body parts, insects lack the appeal of cuddly mammals and birds. They can also bite and sting humans, causing great misery and, occasionally, death. Even the intrepid Lesbian Ranger sometimes curses these small pests while patrolling the beaches of Provincetown (Sand Fleas), traversing the muskeg of Nunavut (Aedes Mosquitoes) or questing for honey in the deep South (Killer Bees). "Drat," she might say, as she tromps resolutely onward, thronged by tiny pursuers.

Insects cause extensive damage to our agriculture and can spread disease. Many plagues and famines of old were the result of these minute, dogged creatures. However, it is important to remember that the insect is merely living her insect life, freely and boldly, and intends no personal malice against you or me. She is intent on survival and sexual congress (not unlike many readers of this text) and, fortunately for our global ecosystem, she is adept at both.

The insect's position on the food chain, as predator of other pests, as fodder for larger animals and as tidiers of carrion and dead vegetation is absolutely essential to the planet's delicate balance. Certainly, without the pollinating benefit of insects,

Flora, as we know her, would no longer exist. In contrast, if humans were to perish, the loss would go largely unnoticed by the crawling, flying and swimming multitudes, with their lapping, chewing and piercing mouth parts. In short, we need them. They do not need us.

Perhaps this is what makes the insect such a compelling organism to study. Many a Lesbian Ranger has remarked that she has been drawn to insects, "like a moth to a flame", their seeming indifference fueling her ardour. The lowly bug's self-assurance and single-mindedness bewitches the helpless researcher, drawing her into wooded glades, sultry swamps and the scintillating field of entomology. Certainly, lesbians and *Insectae* have much in common: feared, misunderstood and unnoticed, we and our creepy-crawly cohabitants possess a tenacious beauty all our own.

When studying insects, it is necessary to afford them all the respect you would a lover. To ensure no permanent damage, J.R. Stevens uses restraint gently and for only short periods of time. The best approach is to observe insects unfettered, in their natural habitats. Take along a notebook and a magnifying glass. If you must move them, encourage them to step onto a leaf or twig of their own volition. As always, a willing subject is more reliable and yields more pleasurable results.

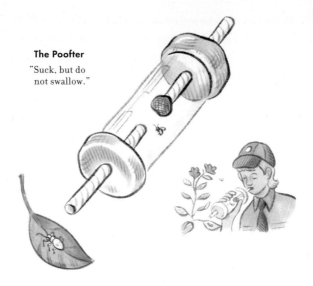

The Poofter

"Suck, but do not swallow."

For closer inspection of small or quick-moving insects, you might want to use a poofter. Named for our auxiliary force of male members, this device allows for companionable observation without molestation.

Do not neglect insects that spend all or part of their lives under water. Remember J.R. Stevens' great luck as she plundered the slough waters! Also keep in mind that insects have different life phases and can assume radically different forms. Upon emergence from the egg, some insects resemble tiny adults. Others look like immature, wingless versions of what they will one day become and are variously named nymphs (if they live on land) or naiads (if they live in water). Worm-like larvae are also young insects. Beetle larvae are fondly called grubs, and fly larvae, maggots. These are transitional stages before adulthood. Butterflies, for example, develop from caterpillars, to pupae, to the gaudy flyers that grace our gardens. This complete metamorphosis is a true Cinderella story, capable of stirring even the most jaded naturalist. Rebirth, in the insect world, abounds! It is because of these inspiring transformations that LNPS has chosen insects to represent Junior Rangers and their clans. Immature bugs so aptly capture the distinct personalities of young womanhood on the path to fruition!

Grub trustworthy friend
Maggot fearless adventurer
Caterpillar inspirer of dreams
Nymph determined leader
Naiad wise wanderer
Larva generous helper

Scientists estimate that there are over 100,000 insect types in North America, many of which have yet to be categorized. In fact, it is estimated that only 3% of insects, globally, have been classified. With this vast number, it is easy to see how a disciplined

METAMORPHOSIS,
OR THE LIFE CYCLE OF AN INSECT.

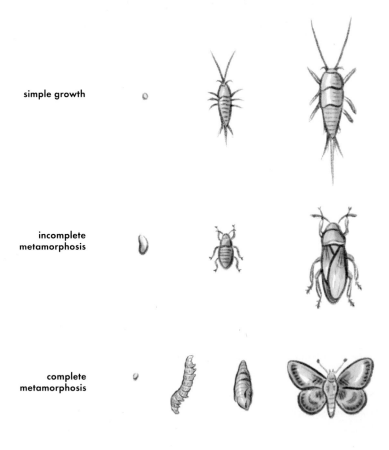

simple growth

incomplete
metamorphosis

complete
metamorphosis

amateur can offer much to the field and, perhaps, even name "a species of her own".

The following is a sampling of some of our most common buzzing brethren. Note that no range maps are provided. These insects play the fields, swamps and forests with gay abandon. In short, they get around, constantly changing their domain. Each has been chosen to represent an insect subtype. Hopefully, these species will stimulate the budding neophyte *and* the experienced entomologist. Whether you are a casual voyeur or a professional scientist, the insect world awaits, in all its glory.

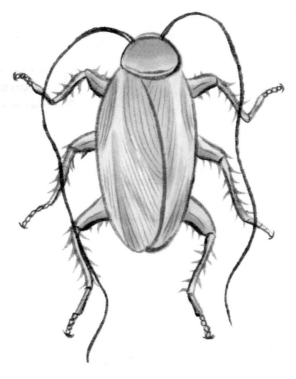

LENGTH Up to 20–45 mm

COLOUR reddish brown
with varied markings

LIFE CYCLE incomplete
metamorphosis

The Cockroach (family *Blattidae*)

Whether you are faintly repulsed by the very name of this insect, or invigorated by its forthright appropriation of a masculine power symbol, the cockroach itself is worthy of study and respect. This sturdy creature is one of the oldest organisms on the planet, dating back 350 million years. Frequently humans have attempted its "control" or eradication, but for naught. This futile effort has resulted in generations of pesticide-resistant survivors, ever more intent upon scurrying out of closets and cracks to feed on crumbs that the dominant culture leaves behind.

The cockroach's determination, ingenuity and sheer numbers strike fear into the hearts of many. True, they sully food with their feces, but otherwise no real threat is posed. They are simply fulfilling their biological destiny. A cockroach is a cockroach is a cockroach — hard shelled and imbued with indomitable perseverance — whether it lurks in the deepest recesses of people's minds or simply runs amok in their pantries.

The Mosquito (family *Culicidae*)

It is a little-known fact that mosquitoes (of which there are many species) feed primarily on nectar and other plant juices. However, when it comes time for the female to create eggs, the gentle aerial-ist is transformed into a protein-dependent predator, roughly thrusting her proboscis willy-nilly into warm flesh. The protective sheath of her labium releases two tubes, edged with cutting tools. These bear down until the skin's surface is pierced and then lubricating, anti-coagulant saliva is pumped into the body while the blood is purloined. When sated, the bloodthirsty insect deposits her cache of genetic material in standing water and resumes the hunt, probing, sucking and laying as many as twenty times in her five-month lifespan. In this way it is possible for an active and ambitious female to create thousands upon thousands of eggs.

One cannot help but admire the daring bloodlust of these winged risk-takers. On any given day, as many as one-third of the world mosquito population may perish. Nonetheless, the female doggedly courts disaster in pursuit of her base appetite, shamelessly and single-mindedly braving chemical foggings and fatal slappings in her eagerness to feast again.

Surprisingly, she does not proceed with stealth. Fearlessly, the female mosquito trumpets her arrival

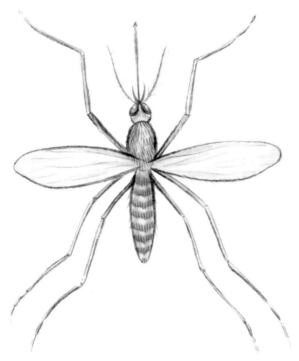

LENGTH up to 10 mm

COLOUR brown, black and grey

LIFE CYCLE complete metamorphosis

DANGER TO THE HOMO
itchy, raised bites, that can spread malaria, yellow
fever, dengue fever and encephalitis

with a distinctive, high-pitched whir. The male
responds to this strident whine by depositing his
sperm in her body, for use at her future convenience.

LENGTH 5–30 mm

COLOUR black with red or yellow markings, glowing green at night

LIFE CYCLE complete metamorphosis

The Firefly (family *Lampyridae*)

Certainly there is no more magical sight than a meadow aglow with fireflies, twinkling like radical fairies in the moonlight! These insects create luminescence in their nether regions by releasing an enzyme, luciferase, which combines with another innate substance, luciferin. The resulting greenish sequence of flashes enables males and females of the same species to locate each other in their nocturnal mating quest. The male firefly will hover in an open area, emitting a specific signal, until a female near the ground responds with her own code. However, despite this advanced communication system, hetero happiness does not always ensue. The females of some species have learned to mimic the light patterns of others. They employ this ruse to lure an amorous male and then devour him, extinguishing his fire forever.

Also called lightning bugs, the firefly belongs neither to the sub-group "fly" nor "true bug". They are beetles, of which there are 300,000 known species. Beetles account for one-quarter of all known creatures. Perhaps it is cleverness, such as that exhibited by the masquerading female, that makes them the most successful organism on earth.

LENGTH queen 20 mm; drone 15 mm; worker female 12 mm

COLOUR black and yellow

LIFE CYCLE complete metamorphosis

BENEFITS TO THE HOMO pollination, honey and beeswax

DANGER TO THE HOMO a nasty sting, used in self-defence (fatal to the worker bee that inflicts it)

The Honeybee (genus *Apoidae*)

Throughout the millennia, the honeybee has provided us with honey, a delicious source of food
energy, and beeswax, essential in the production of
such valuable items as shoe polish, art supplies,
cosmetics, ski wax, candles and the ever-popular
effigies in wax museums. Truly, the honeybee
secretes something for every lesbian! But the most
important contribution these insects make to
humans is pollination of fruit-bearing plants.

Bees live in matriarchal colonies of one queen,
approximately 100 male drones, and up to 60,000
worker females. The queen is responsible for laying
as many as 1,500 eggs every day and is the focal
point of the hive. Drones exist merely to service her
with semen and, after a brief, summer dalliance,
they leave the hive and die.

It is the worker bee who is familiar to most readers, as she is the most outgoing. Worker bees have
different functions, which they intuitively perform
at different times in their life cycles. Whether they
are tending the monarch, building comb, feeding
larvae or guarding the hive, workers are fiercely
loyal and will sacrifice their lives to protect home
and queen. At 21 days of age, they leave the hive to
work the field. Worker bees toil from dawn to dusk,
sucking nectar and nuzzling pollen from as many as

600 flowers in a single outing. The repeated congress with pistils and stamens is satisfying for all and results in food for the bee colony. Nectar is gathered, fanned and aged to make honey, and pollen is stored as the bees' protein source. Hexagonal wax honeycomb preserves these products for future use and is one of the marvels of insect engineering. Even in zero gravity (as witnessed on Space Shuttle missions), bees will construct perfect six-sided combs.

Most fascinating of all is the worker bees' preferred mode of communication. To describe the location and distance of a particularly bountiful stand of flowers, the bees dance, tracing a pattern on the ground and shaking their tails to indicate precise co-ordinates. This characteristic lesbian behaviour (dancing one's intentions) can be traced from the honeybee, through birds, to mammals such as ourselves.

LENGTH 30–70 mm
COLOUR bright green or brown
LIFE CYCLE incomplete metamorphosis

The Katydid (family *Tettigoniidae*)

During summer mating season, the male leaf-green, leaf-shaped insect proudly advertises his conquests by calling "Katy-did, katy-did, katy-did," incessantly. This transparent bravado has provoked many an objective scientist to question the veracity of his claims. After all, every species is comprised of some individuals who are bachelors, some who are prone to mating and some who favour the company of their own kind. This last option is an especially satisfying choice for the female katy-did, well-endowed as she is with a sword-like ovipositor. Perhaps the male betrays some insecurity in his chirp. Perhaps the male is leaf-green with envy. Whatever his motivations, one cannot help but ask, "Katy-did, or katy-didn't?"

The Praying Mantis (family *Mantidae*)

Frequently a lesbian wayfarer is stopped dead in her tracks by the alien beauty of a praying mantis. Bulging eyes protrude from a triangular head, lending a strangely human aspect to the insect; hooked forelegs appear clasped, as if in prayer; and an eerie stillness pervades. However, one would be mistaken to interpret this repose as passivity, meditation or a "live and let live" attitude. The mantis is a finely-tuned killing machine who waits patiently and in absolute immobility for her prey. These can include other mantises, poisonous spiders, wasps and even young mice and birds. The unlucky victim is suddenly grasped in the mantis's "praying hands" before being ripped asunder by the insect's razor-sharp mandibles.

The mantis's prowess in these matters is especially impressive when applied to inept or superfluous lovers. Sometimes a hungry "femme fatale" will interrupt the procreative sex act by devouring her male partner. Wisely, when one appetite is not being satisfied, she sates another. Obviously her communication skills in these matters, though lacking in subtlety, are unparalleled.

There are many varieties of the praying mantis in North America, the most common of which have been imported from Europe and China. The mantis

SIZE 20–150 mm

COLOUR green, brown or grey

LIFE CYCLE incomplete metamorphosis

BENEFITS TO THE HOMO mantises feast on other
pests, and are a favourite of the farmer

is also closely related to the equally fascinating
walking stick (family *Phasmatidae*), a long thin
insect which resembles a twig. Many walking sticks
are spared the high drama of the mantis and reproduce by parthenogenesis (cell-division of
unfertilized eggs.) This so-called "asexual" method
renders lesbian motherhood a breeze.

Camouflage is the primary defence for these
insects. The mantises and walking sticks found in
lush, grassy areas are clad in brilliant green, while
those who live in woodlands favour more sombre
hues, specifically bark-tones.

THE BIRDS AND THE BEES

145

WINGSPAN 75–100 mm

COLOUR orange and black

LIFE CYCLE complete
metamorphosis

The Monarch Butterfly (*Danaus plexippus*)

In no organism is metamorphosis more complete than the *Lepidoptera*, or butterfly. The Monarch, for example, begins its life as an egg and then hatches into a plump, striped, hairless caterpillar. After feasting on ill-tasting milkweed, and hence protecting itself from predators who abhor this flavour, the worm-like larva forms a hard pupa or chrysalis which dangles from the underside of a leaf. It is from this restrictive structure that the gaily clad orange and black butterfly "comes out", dazzling in its new-found beauty, ready to spread its wings and fly, fly, fly! Though it may appear delicate, the experience of self-transformation imbues the butterfly with an inner strength, making it capable of tackling the most daunting challenge.

Like many northern Homos, the Monarch winters in Mexico. Their journey is a perilous one of many thousands of kilometres, flown on paper-thin wings. Miraculously, the insect successfully completes the southbound voyage within weeks and passes a delightful season in the sultry clime. Then, in the spring, she begins the northerly trip, stopping en route to lay her eggs and die. Her offspring hatch, metamorphose and carry on the journey, intuitively following the flight path of their mother and her foremothers before them.

Spiders

LENGTH 2–120 mm, depending upon variety

COLOUR various

DANGER TO THE HOMO all spiders bite, some are poisonous, some fatally so

Ticks

LENGTH 2–10 mm, depending upon variety

COLOUR various

DANGER TO THE HOMO lyme disease is spread by some varieties

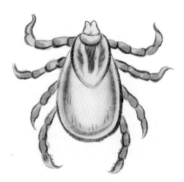

Spiders, Multi-pedes and Their Ilk

(Class *Arachnida*, *Chilopoda* and *Diplopoda*)

Technically, spiders, ticks, mites, centipedes and millipedes are not insects. They may resemble this class of organism because of their diminutive scale and hard exoskeletons, but in fact they lack the requisite six legs and three-part body structure of *Insectae*.

Arachnids, such as the Black Widow Spider and the Deer Tick, are characterized by eight legs, two body-parts and absence of antennae. Spiders also have a pair of fangs attached to poison glands, which they use to inject their prey with venom. This toxin reduces the contents of the victim's body to a liquid, which is then supped on by the eight-legged carnivore. The spider also produces web from its spinnerets to build traps, to wrap egg sacks and, in the case of the Tarantula, to line its burrows. This silken substance is made of protein and is one of the strongest, finest materials found in nature. The spinning and weaving of this fibre, combined with a sharp bite, has long led the spider to be associated with "spinsters" or (to phrase it more scientifically) the female *Homo*. Interestingly, female spiders dominate their male counterparts in size and behaviour, in much the same way the human bull-dyke can dwarf and reduce to snivelling pulp her gay male counterpart.

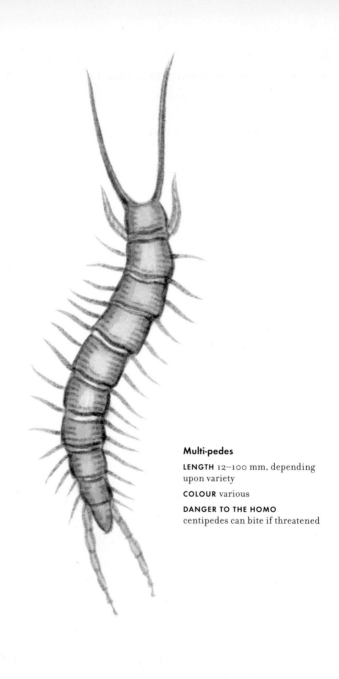

Multi-pedes

LENGTH 12–100 mm, depending
upon variety

COLOUR various

DANGER TO THE HOMO
centipedes can bite if threatened

The tick, another cunning arachnid, lacks the fangs of her spider cousin. However, this absence is in no way debilitating. To feed, she simply thrusts her entire head into the object of her desire, sucking blood until she has grown many times her original size. She may remain on her host for several days before reaching her capacity for sanguinary pleasure. Satisfied and engorged, she withdraws at last, lest she burst apart with the fluids she has ingested.

In contrast, multi-pedes have many body segments and, as their names suggest, many limbs. Centipedes have from 15–181 body parts, each of which is flanked by a pair of legs. Antennae and a pair of poisonous fangs help these creatures locate and kill their insect prey.

Millipedes are very similar but have two sets of legs on each of their body parts and consume plant matter. The mesmerizing undulations of these animals, as they promenade beneath rocks and rotting vegetation, are truly sensuous. However, if disturbed, these earthy creatures will emit a foul smell, curling into a tight ball to protect their delicate undersides.

Feathered Friends

Junior Ranger Betty Ramsay is rarely quiet. This vivacious young woman plays hard and works hard, inspiring others with the song in her heart and the improvised melody on her lips. Why then, as she hikes Ontario's Bruce Trail, is she so uncharacteristically silent? Is she sad, lonely or is there simply no one to talk to?

Despite her garrulous nature, this young scientist knows that the call of a mammal, or insect, or even an amphibian identifies a species and indicates its location as surely as tracks upon new-fallen snow. The crack of a branch or the rustle of leaves also points to an animal with immediate accuracy. J.R. Ramsay is straining to hear aural clues which will lead her to her quarry. Her ears open and attuned to the symphony all around her, she walks stealthily on. She has a goal, and nothing will rout her from her quest.

Betty is a bird-watcher, one of those fiercely determined naturalists poised with pencil, pad and binocular to capture in memory the oft-fleeting sight of feathered beauty. She maintains her "life list" of conquests vigilantly, adding the name and location of each new species she experiences. But Betty demands more than "quantity" from her birding hobby. She also appreciates "quality" and is prepared to spend many patient hours in pursuit of a rare species and its unique and beguiling ways.

Birds are a mystery. Despite our co-existence with them since the dawn of humankind, relatively little is known about these flighty creatures. It seems to J.R. Ramsay that the more she learns, the less she knows. Buck up, Bets! Any worthwhile endeavour always leads to more questions than answers. Ornithology, like all biological explorations, benefits from a legion of lesbians, amateur and professional, spurred on by a common passion, working together toward a common goal.

Where birds are concerned, many obstacles hinder study. Some species migrate many thousands of miles, making it difficult for one birder to experience the full range of their behaviour and habitat. Birds are also very quick creatures, and hence tricky to observe at length and clearly. Finally, all North American *Aves* (birds) are gifted with flight and are able to leave us humans quite literally in the dust.

Nonetheless, bird-watching is the most popular sport in North America, and for good reason, too! These chirpy creatures abound with song, beauty and pluck. The fact that they are able to wing their way effortlessly through the skies (a feat which we can accomplish only in our Freudian dreams) makes any earth-bound lesbian ache with admiration.

THE BIRDS AND THE BEES

153

SPECIALIZED BIRD FEET

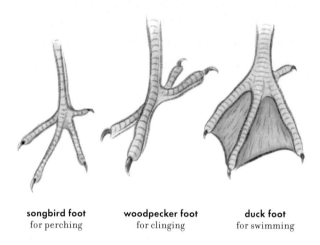

songbird foot
for perching

woodpecker foot
for clinging

duck foot
for swimming

Despite a wide range of behaviour and size, all birds share several characteristics. Species as varied as the rarely seen California Condor (with a wing-span of 2.75 m), and the diminutive Calliope Hummingbird (8 cm), all have beaks, claws, feathers and wings. Each of these body parts is specialized for the habits of its bearer. Some birds grasp, some birds suck, some birds plunge, and nature has developed handy tools to facilitate these tasks.

Birds are able to take to the air by virtue of light-weight, almost hollow bones and intricate feathers used to lift, steer, brake, glide, insulate and protect from the elements. Different species can be identified by plumage (colour and pattern), call, size, shape and flight pattern. A lesbian Turtle Dove seems to bore through the air with rapid strokes, at a rate of up to 80 kilometres an hour. In contrast, hummingbirds hover in one place or even fly backwards. Other birds, like pheasants, prefer a more leisurely glide, whereas others still, like eagles, soar high in the sky on warm air currents.

Bird-watcher Betty keeps her eyes and ears open to this range of traits so that she can determine conclusively which species she is watching. She knows (sadly, from experience) that to fib or erroneously report on one's "life list" may impress others, but lacks the deep satisfaction that comes with successfully spying a truly strange bird or odd duck. With over 800 species in North America, it is easy to make an honest mistake. When possible, try capturing your winged quarry — on camera of course — for closer examination and long-lasting pleasure. Remember, in your zeal to make a positive identification, be careful not to disturb the environment, the bird's nest or the bird herself.

In her many years a-roving, J.R. Ramsay has learned that pursuit is as much fun as conquest. The joy of birding lies in appreciating the habitat as much as the habitant. Betty takes immense satisfaction from the squish of leather boots in fetid earth, the musky odour that rises with each footfall and the sweat of exertion trickling beneath her vest. It all contributes to the gratification which comes from glimpsing a new chick or rare bird.

Sadly, many species have been depleted by habitat loss and the use of pesticides. Birds of prey were greatly jeopardized by the chemical DDT (which weakened eggshells), until its ban in 1972. Fortunately, populations of Brown Pelicans, Bald Eagles, Ospreys and Peregrine Falcons are now rebuilding. However, in the past 100 years some species have been lost entirely, or teeter at the brink of extinction, principally because of hunting. Passenger Pigeons and Eskimo Curlews were slaughtered in the millions for their meat and Whooping Cranes for their feathers. Some scientists fear that songbirds are also approaching disaster because of rapid logging of their summer nesting grounds (boreal forests) and their wintering habitat (tropical rainforests). These sobering facts make the study of birds all the more pressing and spur voracious young birders like Betty onward. She knows that, unless measures are taken to safeguard our feathered friends, fulfilling a "life list" will become a race against time.

On the following pages you will find descriptions of species which are easily found by any spunky amateur. Hopefully they will pique your interest in the thrilling sport of bird-watching. Before you take to the field, however, remember that birds have highly developed senses of hearing and sight. For instance, these perceptive creatures can see the movement of a clock's minute hand with the same clarity with which we perceive the movement of its second hand. Very little escapes their notice! Therefore, in order to get close to birds, be restrained in your dress and in your movements. In this, and all circumstances, sensitivity is generously rewarded.

NOTE: Maps indicate both the summer and winter ranges of migratory birds, and the year-round ranges of non-migratory birds.

THE BIRDS AND THE BEES

LENGTH 53 cm

CALL descending "keer"

COLOUR browns, reds, black and cream

EGGS 2–4, speckled

The Red-Tailed Hawk (*Buteo jamaicensis*)

Contrary to her common name, "Hen Hawk", this noble beast rarely lowers herself to poultry yards. Instead, her tastes run to the wild side. Strong, curved talons are specially designed to hold her squirming prey, while a sharp, curved beak expertly rends flesh. The Red-Tailed Hawk can vary in appearance from reddish-brown to cream-coloured and be marked with a range of patterns. This bird is a tribute to natural diversification within one species and reflects the biological importance of difference. Perhaps because of her adaptability, this high-soaring hawk can be found throughout most of North America.

The Red-Tailed and other hawks, falcons and eagles make excellent sport birds. "Falconry" or "hawking" involves training these animals to hunt. The larger and more intrepid females, all of which are referred to as "falcons", are favoured. Males or "tiercels" are less powerful and aggressive and, therefore, less desirable. Recently, wildlife protection laws have curtailed the numbers of prey-birds taken for this purpose, and the Red-Tailed is grateful. As independent as she is fierce, this hawk prefers to be no man's plaything: she is proud, she is invincible, she is Red-Tailed.

LENGTH 9 cm

CALL high squeak or "chip"

WING-SOUND a high pitched "ze-e-e-e", almost like the buzzing of a bee

MALE COLOUR iridescent green, brown and white with red throat-patch

FEMALE COLOUR brown, olive and white

EGGS 2, white

The Ruby-Throated Hummingbird

(*Archilochus colubris*)

The Ruby-Throated Hummingbird is known for her moves and can fly up, down, forwards and backwards, as she dips her wick in hundreds of flowers each day. This tiny creature is fast, with a racy heart that beats over 1,000 times per minute and wings that beat up to 80 times per second. Her insatiable nectar-sucking has long been the subject of scientific gossip. This small bird is compelled to feed incessantly, lapping up sweet liquids through her straw-like tongue to satisfy her metabolic cravings and fuel her migration to Central America. Twice each summer, she lays two pea-sized eggs. The female raises the chicks alone, and pugnaciously attacks even the largest of predators in defence of her young.

The Ruby-Throated is named solely for the male of the species, characterized by his affected red cravat or gorget (throat patch). Lesbian Ruby-Throated Hummingbirds are more subtly suave. They successfully cruise endless showy flowers while appearing quite discreet themselves.

The Black-Billed Magpie

(*Pica hudsoniana*)

This western bandit is so enthralled by shiny objects she has been known to enter boudoirs in pursuit of booty and even pluck jewels from a lady's body. However, the thievery does not stop here. It is not unusual for a Black-Billed Magpie to tear living flesh from the open wound of a mammal. This black and white bird will also pillage other birds' nests, devouring their eggs and young, and will chase songbirds from food sources. Needless to say, these factors, combined with the bird's loud call and fearless attitude, have earned them and all members of the magpie family a *bad reputation*. Easy enough to acquire in the lesbian world, it is equally hard to dispel. Those of us who have been tarnished with the brush of infamy can well understand how important it is to educate the public about the magpie's virtues, so as to redeem her a place at the hallowed bird feeders of society. She does not benefit from judgment, but understanding. She may be an opportunist, a scavenger and a brat, but there are also other sides to her magpie nature.

This handsome animal's omnivorous diet has many benefits to the larger ecosystem. She devours countless grasshoppers and crickets (insects that can devastate crops). Her taste for carrion moti-

LENGTH 48 cm

CALL various, including harsh "chuck" noises

COLOUR dark iridescent blue/green (almost black) and white

EGGS 7–8, white speckled with brown

vates her to clean up cadavers. And she has been known to dine upon engorged ticks which she has removed from an animal's hide. In short, the Black-Billed Magpie is a helper lesbian, despite her ill-repute.

LENGTH 25 cm

CALL "cheerily cheer up" and "tut tut tut"

COLOUR brown/grey with rusty red breast
and white accents

EGGS 3–7, turquoise

The American Robin *(Turdus migratorius)*

The American Robin has become quite comfortable in suburbia. Her sunny good nature and small bird brain enjoy the comforts and convenience and her highly developed navigational sense keeps her from getting lost, despite a preponderance of cul de sacs and architectural homogeneity.

The merry bird can often be spotted, happily probing the mysteries of lawns and golf courses. With a bounce in her step, she pecks hither and yon, from dawn to dusk, proceeded by her proud, red bosom. She picks up a bit of twine here and rips a worm from the earth there. There are things to do, places to hop and smaller organisms to devour.

This bird feels she has worked hard for widespread distribution, and is now reaping the rewards. She makes herself at home in any ecosystem, from Mexico to the Arctic.

LENGTH 42 cm

CALL "cuk-a, cuk-a, cuk-a"

COLOUR black and white with red on head

EGGS 3–5, white

The Pileated Woodpecker
(*Dryocopus pileatus*)

This *Picidae* (woodpecker) is endowed with a long, hard beak with which it beats a rousing tattoo on ant-infected timber. The unwitting insects are dislodged with the aid of the Pileated's unusually lengthy and prehensile tongue. This appendage has a flinty tip which is barbed, for spearing the prey. Considered together, these anatomical features contribute to form an enviable oral organ.

The drumming action of the bird, whacking wood, also signals a territorial claim to its rivals. In fact, this wood-worker is most easily identified in the bush by the pile-driving "rat-a-tat-tat" of its foraging, as well as its loud rising and falling call. Further evidence of the bird's presence are large, gaping holes which it leaves in vulnerable stumps and trunks.

The male "woody" has more extensive red patches on his head. However, the oft-overlooked female pecker is equally impressive. Both genders stand almost a half-metre tall when erect.

THE BIRDS AND THE BEES

LENGTH 56 cm

CALL "hoot, hoot, hoot-hoot, hoot, hoot"

COLOUR browns, rusts, white, cream and black

EGGS 2–4, white

The Great Horned Owl (*Bubo virginianus*)

This large bird prowls the night on fluffy, almost soundless wings, ever on the look-out for fowl, skunk, mice, porcupine and even house cats. Birds, rodents and pussy are mercilessly devoured in their entirety and then fur and bone are spat up later in the form of a compact pellet.

Hunting is facilitated by extraordinary eyesight. The tufted tuffy can turn her head almost 180 degrees in both directions, in order to vigilantly survey her turf. Perhaps this "all-seeing-ness" is why the ancient Greeks associated owls with Athena, the unmarried goddess of wisdom.

Unfortunately, however, owls have not always been held in such high regard. The Great Horned had a price on her head at different times in North American history. Trained ornithologists worked hard to combat this bounty-hunting, asserting that owls, like all daughters of Nature, have an essential function in the ecosystem. Education has dispelled the bigotry and prejudice of a small-minded public and now the owl is a valued member of most communities.

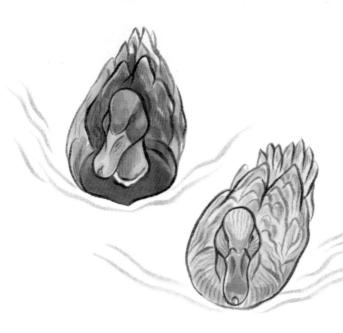

LENGTH 58 cm

CALL female, "quack, quack"; male, a reedy whine

MALE COLOUR iridescent green head, white neck band, brown, black and white body, with patch of blue on each side

FEMALE COLOUR brown, black and white, with patch of blue on each side

EGGS 8–10, pale green

The Mallard Duck (*Anas platyrhynchos*)

The most populous wild duck in the world, Mallards number over 10 million in North America alone. These compact waterfowl are known as "dabblers" because they feed on the surface of the water, ingesting plant and animal material by skimming lakes, rivers and ponds, or by upending to forage below the water line. However, the Mallard also "dabbles" with other birds and is not only the progenitor of the white barnyard duck (with which it will mate), but also the Mallard-Black, Mallard-Gadwall, and Mallard-Pintail hybrids. In this respect, the Mallard is more polyamorously adventurous than most animals and should be applauded for her more-than-welcoming attitude towards other species.

Heterosexual coupling for this open-minded *Anas* is short-lived. After eggs are laid, males abandon their mates to live in secluded bachelor fraternities. At this time males also moult and their distinctive, bright feathers are replaced by brown and white ones, closely resembling those of the female. This transgenderism (eclipse plumage) lasts for over a month, after which time the drakes molt again and return to their colourful selves. Progressive or merely confused, it is plain to see that the Mallard is called a "dabbler" for many reasons.

LENGTH 13 cm

CALL "sweet, sweet, I'm so sweet"

MALE COLOUR brilliant yellow
with some black and white

FEMALE COLOUR olive, black
and white

EGGS 4–6, grey-green, blotched
on wide end

The Yellow Warbler (*Dendroica petechia*)

This gayly coloured bird shows considerable excitement as she hops, flutters and climbs about. A charming socialite, she flits from insect to insect, devouring them all with equal good cheer. Never one for false modesty, this perky songbird warbles, "Sweet, sweet, I'm so sweet." Truer words were never chirped.

Sadly, the destruction of smart perches in well-fashioned old-growth forests is diminishing this species. It seems that pretty, poised and petite lesbians are considered expendable in the interests of profitable logging ventures. However, any woods-woman who has peered into the smartly decorated, milkweed-lined nest, thrilled to the melodious song or spied the attractive busybody preening upon a branch knows better and longs forevermore for but a glimpse of this enchanting creature.

Lower Vertebrates

6

JUNIOR RANGER THIRZA CUTHAND excitedly dons
her crisp, starched uniform and all of the multi-
purpose accessories which adorn it. She has shined
her hiking boots to a mirror polish and, in her
enthusiasm, has also lovingly buffed those of her
fellow Junior Rangers. Cuthand and her troop are
embarking upon an expedition to the snake pits of
Narcisse, Manitoba. Although their journey will be
short and without danger, J.R. Cuthand nonetheless
thrills in anticipation. "Who knows?" she wonders.
"A flat tire might befall us and necessitate an
impromptu sleepover." Like any smart outdoorswoman, she is preparing for all eventualities. She
knows that within the complex, pack-like dynamic
of the Corps she is not a leader. However, as a
cheerfully submissive Junior Ranger, there is much
she can, and does, contribute. Perhaps this explains
her strong empathy with other so-called bottoms:

amphibians, reptiles and fish. Thirza knows that these evolutionary precursors to warm-blooded birds and mammals are not merely biological stepping stones to higher life forms. They are complex beings in their own right and richly deserve our attentions.

For too long our hairless buddies have been stigmatized, overlooked or treated with callous indifference. J.R. Cuthand understands that these attitudes are born of ignorance but still they make her blood boil! Her experience in the lesbian bush has taught her that the mighty — be they a towering Grizzly or the bossy girl in her pack — cannot exist without the presence of others, perhaps smaller or more passive, to dominate.

The web of life involves mutually beneficial interchanges of power which together form a fabric. Each of us is part of its warp and woof, spunky protozoa and *Homo sapiens* alike. We are all interdependent and lower vertebrates, with their vast numbers, ranges and variation of behaviour, are no exception.

Amphibians

SOMETIMES, in her passionate pursuit of amphibious beings, Junior Ranger Lee Piu-Ming is brought up short by the very mystery of life. As an avid amateur herpetologist, she knows that all vertebrates evolved from aquatic creatures. At one point we *Homos*, like the inky tadpole, struggled to sprout legs, ached to breathe air and reached boldly, irrepressibly forward, drawing ourselves onto dry land. The fierce bravery of our ancestors, as they took those small yet mighty steps — toes splayed and gills a-flapping — stirs in J.R. Lee a deep respect for the interconnectedness of all living things. As she goes about her research, peering into stagnant pool and parting damp leaf-rot, her heart-strings quiver with the knowledge that what she seeks is really our own human past.

The term amphibian means "two lives", referring to the creature's predilection to live both underwater and upon *terra firma*. These bi-habitat animals are characterized by moist, scale-less skin which is permeable to both water and oxygen. A significant amount of cutaneous respiration occurs and is essential for lungless varieties (such as most salamanders) or when gill-less amphibians are submerged.

The skins of newts, salamanders, frogs and toads also contain numerous glands, some of which secrete an amphibian aphrodisiac, and others which emit a defensive poison or odour. J.R. Lee learned the importance of always washing one's hands after touching amphibians when she relieved herself after physically examining a salamander. The burning sensation in her loins was the result of more than a deep-seated interest in biology. Fortunately, J.R. Lee's heart is as tender as her private parts and she embraced the experience as a valuable lesson in empathy. She realized that the insect repellent and sunblock on her hands were no doubt equally troubling to the thin-skinned salamander. She vowed, henceforth, to wash before *and* after fondling these small animals and, inspired by her sterling example, you should likewise do the same.

In some amphibian species, eggs are laid by the female and then subsequently fertilized by the male. In others, sperm is deposited by the male and then taken up by the female. Either way, penetrative sex between genders is usually omitted. Whether they engage in these highly evolved customs or resort to more primitive means, the genetic material is always deposited in water or moist soil.

Amphibians usually undergo metamorphosis in their development from jelly-like egg to adult. Amphibious larvae, or tadpoles, more closely resemble fish than their progenitors. These small, swimming creatures live in water, subsisting initially on vegetation and later on animal products, until their legs are formed and they are ready to take their place upon dry land.

Once they emerge from the murky depths of adolescence, all amphibious adults are carnivorous, and some, cannibalistic. These small animals are usually busiest at night when the air is damp with possibility.

There are 250 species of amphibians in North America, many of which are at risk from ultraviolet radiation, pollution, acid rain and the decimation of wetlands. Some naturalists fear that the genetic modifications appearing in these animals foreshadow fatal anomalies which will begin to appear in larger lesbians such as ourselves. It is important that more in-depth study of amphibians is conducted and that we each take special care not to disturb, injure, capture or kill our moist and slippery sisters.

What follows is a sampling of clammy creatures, chosen for the ways in which they represent the variety of *Amphibia* found on this continent.

LENGTH 5–11 cm

COLOUR brown, grey, rust or olive with patches of yellow or beige, dark spots and yellow or orange warts

The American Toad (*Bufo americanus*)

A voracious consumer of insects, the American Toad possesses powerful limbs and an even more powerful sense of entitlement. This, combined with a "hop to it" attitude, has enabled it to colonize the entire eastern part of the continent, with the exception of the southern lowlands (Rebel Toad territory). This plump, wart-covered amphibian is characterized by a light line down the centre of its back and a loud 30 second trill. The call of the American Toad is rarely confused with the short, pithy song of its Canadian cousin. Generally smaller and paler, the Canadian Toad is steeped in the ironic marshlands of the prairies.

All toads possess a pair of Bidder's organs. These rudimentary gonads will grow into functional ovaries, on either gender, if the existing reproductive organs are damaged. This unique, naturally occurring default-to-femaleness (and MTF transgenderism) helps to ensure species survival.

LENGTH 2–5 cm

COLOUR green, tan or black, often with dark spots

The Pacific Tree Frog (*Hyla regilla*)

The Pacific Tree Frog can be found from British Columbia to California, in low-lying coastal areas and on mountains at altitudes up to 3,000 metres. However, it is her prevalence around Hollywood which has led to fame. Film and television have appropriated her unique "ribbit, ribbit" call to signify amphibious life everywhere and her form is ubiquitous in children's shows and advertising. Visually, the starlet is identified by variable colouration (to co-ordinate with her environment), long, dainty toes ending in round pads and a dark line through her eyes. Her use in media is not surprising, considering the Pacific Tree Frog's pretty, feminine form. However, despite audience recognition, the actual benefits to the Pacific Tree Frog have been few. Like all amphibians, this ground-dweller suffers habitat destruction at a frightening rate.

LENGTH 9–20 cm

COLOUR mottled green, yellow or grey with white belly

The Bullfrog (*Rana catesbeiana*)

The Bull-Dyke Frog is capable of conquering all manner of insects, fish, reptiles, other amphibians and even small birds and baby ducks. Her propensity for young meat can be distasteful, but seems to be part of her innate predatory nature. Often massive in size, she is characterized by her distinctive "jug o' rum" mating call, produced by inflating the vocal sack in her neck. Needless to say, a group or "hockey team" of Bull-Dykes can create quite a din, each competing for prominence by asserting "jug o' rum, jug o' rum, jug o' rum" more loudly than the last. This mighty bellowing can be heard at a distance of half a kilometre.

The sheer bulk of these amphibians and their long, muscular hind limbs have led to their introduction in many non-indigenous areas as a source of frog-legs. Lesbian biologists will not be surprised to learn that these efforts at domestication have failed and the adaptable Bull has escaped and flourished. The Bull Frog now populates much of America and Hawaii.

LENGTH 20–43 cm

COLOUR grey or rusty with maroon gills and blue spots

The Mudpuppy (*Necturus maculosus*)

Many of us have been accused of arrested development, however we are not without biological precedent. Non-transforming amphibians, and particularly the youthful Mudpuppy, aptly illustrate that the "Peter Pan syndrome" is a valued part of nature. The nocturnal Mudpup remains in its larval or tadpole stage, never leaving lakes and streams to venture forth onto dry land. Whether this is because life is so good as a larva, or so bad as an adult, is not known. However, it does illustrate that youth is not merely transitional but a significant life-stage in its own right.

This mid-continental sea monster is endowed with a long, eel-like body flanked by stubby legs and deep-red feathery gills. The waterdog exuberantly trolls the freshwater depths, feeding upon worms, insects and fish. The Mudpuppy reaches its full size and sexual maturity at the age of six years and never regrets foregoing onerous adult responsibilities such as breathing.

LOWER VERTEBRATES

LENGTH 5–10 cm

COLOUR enamel-white belly with black spots, brownish back

The Four-Toed Salamander
(*Hemidactylium scutatum*)

The most valuable asset of this amphibian is its delicious and detachable rear end. Like some of the other lungless salamanders, this small creature has the ability to relinquish its tail when bitten. The predator becomes distracted by the twitching posterior and the spotted tease can escape to regenerate the missing part.

Mating between these sphagnum-dwellers is particularly efficient. Called a "tail walk", the female rubs her snout against the base of the male's tail. This results in sperm being deposited on the ground to be picked up by the female at her leisure. Fertilized eggs are subsequently laid and, in an unusual amphibian display of maternalism, aggressively guarded by the mother.

LENGTH 13–22 cm

COLOUR brown or black
with yellow or orange
belly

The Roughskin Newt (*Taricha granulosa*)

The Roughskin Newt engages in behaviour known to biologists as "flashing". These bold creatures arch their backs when disturbed, lifting their fore-bodies and tails to display their startlingly bright orange or yellow bellies. Many a predator is embarrassed by this shameless display of private underparts and leaves the exhibitionist unscathed.

This salamander lurks in moist woods, boggy grasslands and wells of loneliness along the west coast.

Reptiles

THERE WAS A TIME when reptiles dominated the earth, and were larger and more powerful than terrestrial beasts before or since. These immense vertebrates evolved from amphibians but had a distinct advantage: their hard-shelled eggs ably protected their young and could be laid far from water. As the great seas receded, the cold-blooded behemoths crawled from the ooze, overtaking land and skies. Masterfully and proudly, they reigned the globe for over 200 million years.

Many a Junior Lesbian Ranger thrills to learn about these commanding giants who were capable of shaking the earth with their very footfalls. The long-standing supremacy of these titans makes them compelling subjects of study. However, as the Rangers are quick to point out, "Present-day reptiles are tops, too!". Fascinating communities of crocodiles, alligators, turtles, tortoises, snakes and lizards continue to abound. In fact there are over 300 species indigenous to North America, 21 of which are venomous. Reptiles remain worthy of our respect, and our caution!

Though some reptiles may resemble amphibians at first glance, more intimate examination reveals many notable deviations. Junior Ranger E.A. Hobart is a whiz at this differentiation, having studied the

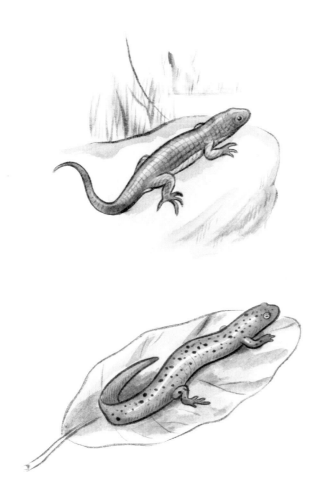

Typical Reptile and Amphibian
Can you tell the difference?

confusing bisaurus for many years. Fortunately she outgrew this tortured passion and is now an experienced herpetologist, equally practised with the horny lizard and the silky salamander. Like all conscientious lesbian-lovers, she knows that correct identification is the first step towards truly getting to know a species. She has generously agreed to share her expertise by compiling a handy chart designed to assist in the study of amphibians and reptiles.

REPTILES	AMPHIBIANS
vertebrae (backbone)	
cold-blooded (inability to regulate body temperature)	
regular regeneration and shedding of skin	
dry, scaly skin	moist, smooth, permeable skin
no respiration through skin	respiration through skin
claws	no claws
no gills	gills while young; sometimes into adulthood
external ear openings	no external ear openings
internal fertilization	external fertilization
hard-shelled eggs laid on land	jelly-like eggs laid in water
young like miniature adults	young transition through a larval or tadpole stage

For this, and the contributions of all our Junior Rangers, we are deeply grateful. Pants off to you, J.R. Hobart!

It is important to note that all life exists on a spectrum. As we have seen, some amphibians remain in the larval stage for their entire lives and more closely resemble fish than an adult frog or salamander. In contrast, others spend their complete life-cycle on land, much like their reptilian brethren. Likewise, reptiles such as the aptly named Earless Lizard have no external ear openings and, in this way, seem more akin to amphibians. Others, like the Copperhead Snake, give birth to live young, a trait which is usually thought to be mammalian. Categories such as *Reptilia* and *Amphibia* are artificial constructions, created to group organisms for the purpose of study. Nature does not adhere to such narrow-minded bounds and constantly challenges us with her healthy diversity.

Even within a single species there can be such variety of behaviour and form that it is difficult to believe that two individuals are genetically the same. For example, Milksnakes can be red, striped with yellow and black. However, they can also be beige, patched with brown and black spots. Milksnakes clearly illustrate that exceptions are as common as generalities and that, in nature, "Deviation is the rule". Like this legless example, we are all actively engaged in the process of evolution and hence are ever-changing. Norms are not "normal" but briefly existing patterns in the ongoing history of biology.

As you study the following examples of reptilian life, admire the predatory and defense mechanisms exhibited by each. Though *Reptilia* have slid from world domination, they nonetheless remain masters of survival. These critters crawl over our continent, from marshlands to deserts, beaches to plains, and are an intricate and integral part of Nature, enriching the lives of all outdoorswomen who are fortunate enough to witness their scaliness.

TYPES OF SCALES

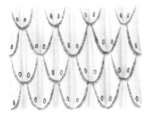

keeled and pitted
(found on snakes)

keeled
(found on
spiny lizards)

smooth and round
(found on skinks)

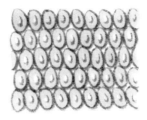

granular
(found on the
limbs of many lizards)

LENGTH 16—24 cm

COLOUR rusty brown
or black with
white/bluish throat
and underside

The Desert-Grassland Whiptail
(*Cnemidophorus uniparens*)

Their long, whip-like tails and penchant for speed make these reptiles, and the larger whiptail family, compelling to the lesbian observer. Certainly, few have experienced these small, stream-lined lizards and not longed to know more about their lifestyle. How do they spend their active days? And where do they spend their whip-tailed nights?

Although much research remains undone, biologists have established a startling fact about these organisms, which might explain their attraction for those of our ranks. The Whiptail is an all-girl species. Each spring, the exclusively female population each lays one to four fertile (though unfertilized) eggs, which hatch into more self-sufficient females. Once, male Whiptails were present, but are now unnecessary and simply do not exist.

This Amazon subsists primarily on insects. Her female independence is flanked by six or seven light stripes and is guided by common sense organs, principally a long and deeply forked tongue.

The Short-Horned Lizard

(*Phrynosoma douglassi*)

This lizard is often erroneously called a "Horny Toad", despite the fact that it is clearly a reptile and not an amphibian. However, the Short-Horned male, like all lizards and snakes, is gifted with unique sexual prowess. These well-endowed creatures embody the theory that "two heads are better than one", especially when it comes to reproduction. Two sexual organs, or hemipenes, are used one-at-a-time for penetration. The benefits of this two-pronged approach (though baffling to the scientific establishment) are satisfying to ponder. The presence of an extra erect and willing organ is no doubt on the wish-list of many females who wonder why double dongs are not adopted by more species.

Characterized by a prominent armour of scaly horns and spikes, the plump Short-Horned Lizard is flawlessly camouflaged against sandy, rocky terrain. However, members of this species are sometimes forced to actively defend themselves. When threatened, these ant-eating lizards will burst blood vessels in the corners of their eyes and shoot a stream of blood up to one metre. Blood is rarely used as a weapon in nature and is therefore startlingly effective. Those of us who menstruate

LENGTH 6–15 cm

COLOUR grey, yellow, brown or rusty with 2 rows of dark spots on back

can well imagine the power and efficacy of squirting our tormentors with a well-aimed shot of monthly drippings.

LENGTH 2–5.7 m

COLOUR dark grey or black;
young are black with yellow bands

The American Alligator

(*Alligator mississippiensis*)

Though we at LNPS appreciate a femme's finery, we nonetheless believe that making handbags from a fellow lesbian is highly inappropriate. Fortunately, legislation is now in place to protect the American Alligator from heinous hide-hunters and these magnificent creatures are beginning to make a come-back. This is important to the ongoing survival of many species because the Alligator digs deep, wide pits for mud-wallowing. Rather than mere self-indulgence, this dirty little habit creates reservoirs in which other animals can drink and feed.

Despite her well-earned reputation as a man-eater, the American Alligator subsists primarily on fish, small mammals, amphibians, snakes and turtles. As nurturing as she is fatale, this, the largest North American reptile, is a devoted parent. The female buries her eggs in a guarded mound, un-covering the hatchlings at birth and carrying them to water in her mouth. The young remain at her side from one to three years, where they are taught the intricacies of the hunt.

LENGTH 70 cm
COLOUR grey
RANGE Atlantic Ocean

The Atlantic Ridley Sea Turtle
(*Lepidochelys kempi*)

Every year or two, these hard-shelled, heart-shaped love machines paddle thousands of miles from the feeding grounds of the northern Atlantic to a site of group sexual activity off the coast of Mexico.

At one time, as many as 40,000 libertines would romp together in the shallows. Like many travellers to southern climes, they would abandon themselves wholly to their polyamorous pleasures, coupling frequently and indiscriminately. If male members were in short supply, no matter. Female turtles can access previously acquired sperm stored in their bodies for up to seven years. With or without recent insemination, fertilized eggs were laid on the southern beach where the females themselves were hatched.

Sadly, however, the Ridley's sexual stamina and reproductive resourcefulness has led to its eggs being hunted as aphrodisiacs. This, combined with drownings in shrimp nets, has decimated the population of gay fornicators to the verge of extinction. Indeed all sea turtles, of all orientations, are now in jeopardy.

LENGTH 10–25 cm

COLOUR olive or
black with red and
yellow accents

The Painted Turtle (*Chrysemys picta*)

Wild basking turtles in the eastern wetlands frolic and romp, sunning themselves in great reptilian stacks, on rocks and logs protruding from ponds. This habit of piling on top of each other is a playful, pleasurable pastime which at times reaches orgiastic heights.

Sadly, not all turtles are able to express their natures in such a consenting and unfettered manner. The Painted Lady Turtle is often confined to compromising situations such as pet stores. There are those who want to buy her, put her into glass houses of infamy (aquaria) and touch her — use her as their cold-blooded toy. Not surprisingly, she often retreats into herself (for the sake of self-preservation), withdrawing into carapace (upper shell) and plastron (belly plate). These bony casings form an excellent defence for all world-weary turtles and tortoises.

The female of the species is larger than the male (as in most sub-aquatic turtles) and both are characterized by bright facial markings.

LENGTH 35–40 cm

COLOUR sandy and rusty browns

The Gopher Tortoise
(*Gopherus polyphemus*)

The Gopher is the only tortoise found in North America. This proverbially slow and steady earth mother uses her flat fore-limbs and stumpy hind legs to dig burrows up to ten metres in length, which are hospitably shared with insects, snakes, frogs, raccoons, opossums and Burrowing Owls. Not surprisingly, she is a vegetarian, and values her independence too much to cohabit with a mate. She becomes only more idiosyncratic with time and can live for over 50 years.

Though some may laugh at this earnest fossil from another era, the Gopher Tortoise is a "key" species and many others are dependent upon her for their survival. Unfortunately, this animal is threatened by habitat destruction because of human development and, as a result, her entire community is at risk.

LENGTH 45–125 cm

COLOUR varying combinations of black, brown, grey, yellow and/or beige

The Common Garter Snake
(*Thamnophis sirtalis*)

Like the sock garters worn by Lesbian Rangers on formal occasions, Garter Snakes are longitudinally striped.

In the northlands, these highly successful reptiles winter communally, awaking to a roiling orgy in the spring. A kinetic "breeding ball" of males, up to one metre in diameter, encircles a single female. Sometimes a frolicsome male will impersonate female characteristics to lure its brethren to its own flesh. This naturally occurring drag act is just part of the merry hijinks to be found in a snake pit, home of thousands of long and lusty individuals.

Garter Snakes are the most wide-ranging snakes in North America and frequently can be found near water, in forests, marshes or meadows. Although they revel in body-to-body contact, they do not appreciate being woman-handled. When displeased, they emit a malodorous musk and can, on occasion, bite. Outdoorswomen should be content with fondling their discarded skins, which the snake strips two or three times a year.

LENGTH 36–84 cm

COLOUR olive, reddish, beige or brown

The Rubber Boa *(Charina bottae)*

This is the most primitive of North American snakes and still carries vestigial hind legs resembling spurs on either side of the anus. The smooth, stubby snake is almost blind and senses paramours and prey with a series of highly sensitive heat-pits around its lips, which pinpoint the precise location and distance of its victim.

Like its South American relations, the Anaconda and the Boa Constrictor, the Rubber kills birds, rodents and other reptiles by suffocating them in its muscular coils. This aggressive hug is followed by a deep-throated swallow of the entire organism.

Something Fishy

SOME LESBIANS ESCHEW large, warm-blooded wildlife; some forswear sticky or sinuous belly-sliders; some turn away from the beauty of birds. These queer nature-lovers, though few in number, are called for a higher — or lower — purpose. Unwilling to accept a hierarchical approach to classification, they pursue their passion without shame. A fever burns within them, incomprehensible to many, and yet refusing to yield to social convention or censure. Spurred on by a love of science and a commitment to their chosen field, they plunge into fieldwork. Despite all obstacles, they persevere, driven mercilessly by the sight, the sound, yea, even the smell of their obsession: freshwater fish of North America.

Sadly, as with most of this guidebook, limitations of size mean we can give only the most cursory attention to these many and varied species. Although this will greatly disappoint the committed fish-lover, perhaps it will encourage others to conduct their own research. The efforts of many ichthyologists are needed to part the waters of ignorance that surround these ancient creatures.

Most readers are familiar with the flesh of fish, particularly that which has graced their tables. But there is so much more to learn about these delicious species.

Some families, such as the pike and pickerel (*Esocidae*), have reputations of great cunning and courage and have earned the nickname "river wolf". Others, such as sturgeons (*Acipenseridae*), are renowned for their great age (up to 70 years) and size (up to three metres). Some, like the carp (*Cyprinidae*), have evolved creative physiognomy and have teeth in their throats instead of their mouths. Others, like the salmon (*Salmonidae*), have vast ranges and migrate thousands of kilometres from fresh to salt water and back again.

Likewise, in the sexual realm, there is a delicious range of fishiness. Hermaphroditic glands are found in some perches and darters (*Percidae*) and basses (*Percichthyidae*), allowing for what one can only imagine being remarkably self-satisfying self-fertilization. In other basses, transgenderism is the rule. These slippery creatures begin life as male and then grow up: into females. Males of the catfish (*Ictaluridae*) and sunfish (*Centrarchidae*) families take on so-called female traits by tending the eggs and young. Some might see this behaviour as gender dysphoric mimicry but we at LNPS prefer to regard it as responsible parenting. For some fish, procreation demands penetration. However, for most it is as clean and simple as two sexes swimming side by-side while shedding genital emissions. These meldings of genetic material can be very liberal.

For example, trout (*Salmonidae*) have hybridized (cross-bred) so extensively that the number of sub-species is truly innumerable.

Despite these progressive predilections, fish are not all fun and games. Some can pose danger to the biologist and angler alike and should be handled with caution. Pike and pickerel, as noted, are fearlessly aggressive and have many sharp teeth. They will not hesitate to bite viciously and may even see your small, tender body-parts as attractive prey. Walleye and perch both have sharp dorsal fins capable of badly wounding human flesh and should be handled gingerly. The Bullhead, a type of catfish, can also cause great discomfort. Its scaleless skin is covered with a toxic mucus (similar to some amphibians) and its fins contain poisonous spines. As it lives at the bottom of murky, shallow streams, care should be taken to avoid wading barefoot. Remember, waterproof protection in the form of good old-fashioned rubbers is stylish, health-conscious and identifies you as a responsible troller. Most lesbians will never need them but they are nonetheless important to consider, especially when verging on a slippery slope. Accidents can happen to even the most committed lesbian bush-woman.

Despite the magnificent range of anatomy and sexual practice found within this fishy class of organism, there are some common features. Of the 600 species in North America, all have fins for swimming, gills for breathing, a flexible backbone and an inability to regulate body temperature. Most are also covered with scales: small, hard plates that protect the vulnerable flesh.

Fish are the oldest form of vertebrate life and account globally for over 40% of backbone-bearing creatures. Some of these cold-blooded animals are traditionalists and have changed relatively little since prehistoric times, whereas others have evolved and mutated with wanton abandon.

Open-Mouthed Bass
a typical fish

To date, much behavioural data has been collected by sport fisherwomen and, although valuable, it lacks the subtlety and depth acquired through long-term scientific study. Thanks to anglers, fish stocks have been introduced far outside their natural ranges, increasing the availability of this tender meat. However, our insatiable appetites do not necessarily serve the ongoing viability of our underwater sisters and their worlds. Herein lies the central dilemma in lesbian conservation: how to fulfill the unbridled desires of the *Homo*, while respecting the needs of other lesbian species. Some sportswomen have found a personal solution to this conundrum. Rather than hanging up their sleek, black hip-waders forever, they continue to fish, gently returning their catches to water, unharmed thanks to barbless hooks. These outdoorswomen take pleasure from these encounters — woman and fish brought together by the vicissitudes of fate, sharing a watersport in time before carrying on, alone, richer for the experience.

Flora, Special Friend to Fauna

7

WE AT LESBIAN NATIONAL PARKS and Services think of Flora and Fauna as two women in a co-dependent relationship. Each is as vital to the other as sunlight, air and water and neither can move a muscle without "making waves".

Not surprisingly, these life-mates have had their share of ups and downs, diffculty and strife. In coupledom there is a myriad of implications and consequences to even the slightest variation in behaviour. This tiresome fact of lesbian life has been experienced by plants and animals for millions of years. For example, the delicate balance of Nature is such that a shift in insect population can destroy vegetation, or a propagation of a certain type of plant can significantly change bird or amphibian behaviour. One can only imagine the resentment that this long, conjoined history has wrought! And yet somehow the animal and vegetable worlds persevere, together.

The relationship between Flora and Fauna is, in fact, most vulnerable to outside forces such as weather. The capricious malice of droughts, blizzards and squalls devastates plants and animals alike. However, it is human interference (a treacherous variable in any lesbian relationship) that wreaks the greatest havoc. Entire ecosystems have been effectively obliterated by man's awesome ignorance and greed and many, many species rendered extinct. There may well come a point when the checks and balances developed by Flora and Fauna will no longer compensate for this wanton destruction and their dynamic relationship will erode beyond repair, through no fault of its committed partners.

Fortunately, plants and animals are gifted with a remarkable ability to evolve, particularly in response to environmental conditions. Neither Flora nor Fauna are stick-in-the-muds, despite the upheaval which invariably comes with change. Perhaps this is what keeps the age-old relationship spicy: the constant reinvention and refinement of their multiple identities through evolutionary deviance, anomaly and sexual selection.

In this primal dance, the reader might be surprised to learn that Flora (often characterized as passive) is firmly on top. Plants capture and store energy from the sun and, in doing so, provide energy for all living things. This miraculous process, photosynthesis, is the basis of life. Without it, all living organisms would not and could not exist. Plants are the foundation of the food chain and manufacturers of that heady drug, oxygen. As well as providing the very stuff of being, they also furnish lesbians with shelter (wood), reading material (paper), heat (fossil fuels) and pharmaceuticals (digitalin, morphine, etc.). Truly, Flora's gifts are profound and unending.

Earth would be unrecognizable without this bounty, and Fauna knows it. She may strut and roar but ultimately she realizes that Flora firmly holds the reins. It is Flora who resolutely drives their relationship and the future of this planet.

Trees

THE TREE IS MORE than an oversized plant. It is a symbol of life, family and knowledge. These magnificent beings, which are so much a part of human history and mythology, are the oldest living things on earth. The Bristlecone Pines of the Rocky Mountains, for example, achieve an age of over 6,000 years. Some of these trees, living today, have existed since before the advent of written language, use of the wheel and the birth of Judaism.

By studying the physical structure of these organisms, we can learn more about their function and, through the power of metaphor, ourselves as well.

All trees, including the 800 species found in North America, are supported at their foundation by an intricate web of roots which gather water and minerals from the soil and secure the tree to the ground. Usually this subterranean system is as extensive as the tree's foliage. What we see above the ground, be it an Arctic Dwarf Willow or a 12,000 ton Sequoia, is only half the picture.

Junior Ranger Megan Richards has no trouble envisioning this underground support system. She knows that her emotional well-being depends upon a complex tangle of relationships, to girlfriends, ex-girlfriends, ex-girlfriends' girlfriends, ex-girlfriends' ex-girlfriends and girlfriends' ex-girlfriends (not

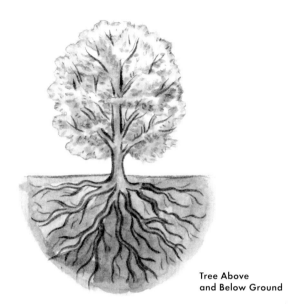

**Tree Above
and Below Ground**

to mention their pets). Together, these women nourish and anchor J.R. Richards and are the basis of an often unacknowledged chosen-family "tree". Likewise, the root structure of a stately Live Oak or gnarled Pitch Pine, though unseen, is an integral and essential component of its being.

Out of this underground web emerges the tree trunk. It rises from the soil, a single, woody stalk supporting a crown of branches adorned with leaves, scales or needles. The central stem can be as large as 12 metres in diameter and is comprised of an inner core of dead heartwood, an outer ring of new sapwood (carrying water and nutrients) and a

CROSS-SECTION OF A TREE TRUNK

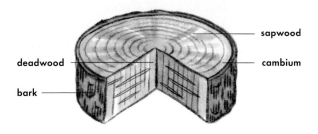

protective sheath of bark. Essentially, the centre of the trunk is dead as a doornail. As Junior Ranger Deborah Kelly is quick to point out, the same can be said of many political movements and even society itself. It is the outer fringes which carry the lifeblood of progress, whereas the old, conservative centres of power are devoid of vitality. Tree trunks, like social structures, grow and change due to activity on the margins.

This development occurs in two directions. The tips of twigs lengthen and create branching, while cambium cells just beneath the bark cause the trunk, branches, twigs and roots to grow thicker. In climates such as North America, this growth takes place in warmer months. A slightly darker line is created at the point at which the yearly growth spurt ends, making it possible for us to accurately assess the age of a tree by counting the rings. Though we at Lesbian National Parks and Services endeavour to avoid ageism (we do not bisect recruits to determine their years!), age identification can be useful in getting to know an organism better. Establishing the age of a tree can also help us develop an historical profile of a region.

Leaves and needles manufacture food for a tree. Photosynthesis is the process by which green chlorophyll transforms sunlight, water, minerals and carbon dioxide into carbohydrates and oxygen. The large surface area of leaves, covered with minute pores called stomata, allows for the passage of gases necessary in this chemical process.

$$CO_2 + H_2O \rightarrow [CH_2O] + O_2$$

Photosynthesis in trees and all plants is the most basic "cooking and cleaning" mechanism of the planet. Food energy is created, seemingly from an empty refrigerator, as water molecules are split and tidied into oxygen and hydrogen, the latter of which reacts with carbon dioxide to create sucrose, starch and cellulose. Though this leafy labour is fundamentally responsible for feeding the planet, it is rarely given its due. Like most food preparation, it is deemed too base — too simple — to warrant mention. Yet without photosynthesis we simply would not exist.

All trees are either hermaphroditic or single-sexed. Interestingly, differentiated "male" or "female" trees are quite recent in evolutionary terms. The earliest trees were endowed with two sets of sex organs and, to this day, these specimens are the most reproductively successful. In contrast, Johnny-come-lately "male" trees have no real function once pollen is produced. They do not make seeds to propagate the species but they do take up valuable space, water and minerals.

In many North American cities, "male" single-sexed trees predominate. Landscapers have eschewed "females" on the grounds that they are messy (fallen fruit) or smelly. Indeed, some female trees have a distinct odour which attracts pollinators to their flowers. But the idea that this perfume is unpleasant, or that the resulting female fruits are untidily juicy, sounds like all-too-familiar sexism to an enlightened outdoorswoman. As well as being gender biased, "male" plantings create a profusion of pollen which have contributed to the explosion of asthma on this continent.

monoecious	"male" and "female" flowers grow on the same tree; some self-pollinate, and some need another monoecious tree with which to pollinate
dioecious	"male" and "female" reproductive parts develop on different trees

Conifers

THE MIGHTY REDWOOD towers to an erect height of
over 100 metres while maintaining impressive
girth. This thrusting trunk is surrounded by an
ample profusion of soft, flat needles. There are no
showy flowers here, nor are they needed. The great
Redwood is a "sister doing it for herself". Her seeds
are produced single-handedly and spread with
great abandon from hundreds of protective cones
which litter the forest floor. Her range may be limited to coastal California and Oregon, but the
Sequoia sempervirens is known far and wide, inspiring us all with her majesty.

This, the emblematic tree of Lesbian National
Parks and Services, is but one example of the end-
lessly fascinating conifers (cone-bearers). These
great trees have existed for hundreds of millions of
years and have been used to celebrate pagan rites,
such as Christmas, since the dawn of humankind.
Most conifers keep their needles or scales all year
long and, for this reason, are often called "ever-
greens". Also referred to as "non-flowering trees",
conifers actually grow cones from flower-like
organs. Smaller, pollen-producing cones are found
on lower branches and larger egg-cell-producing
cones are found on upper branches. The sex act
itself is facilitated by friendly breezes, which bring

The Redwood
Symbol of the Force

the genetic material together. When fertilized, the egg cells replicate into seeds, which are released from cones upon maturity or optimum environmental conditions. Some trees, such as the Lodgepole Pine, rely on the heat of forest fires to open the cone. Most other pines release their seeds only when it is hot and dry. Because the cones will close up again if it becomes humid, it is possible to foretell the weather by observing their movements.

This happily self-sufficient system of reproduction has served the conifers well. With over 100 species in North America, these hardy, hermaphroditic trees cover the northland and can be found from coastal rainforests to mountain peaks.

Longleaf Pine cone responding to humidity

COMMONLY FOUND SPECIES INCLUDE:

true pines (*Pinus*)	Red Pine, Longleaf Pine, Ponderosa Pine, Lodgepole Pine, Scotch Pine, Sugar Pine, etc.
spruces (*Picea*)	White Spruce, Blue Spruce, Engelmann Spruce, etc.
cedars (*Libocedrus*)	Incense Cedar, Northern White Cedar, etc.
junipers (*Juniperus*)	Common Juniper, Eastern Red Cedar, etc.

Broadleaf Trees

WHO CAN RESIST A FRUIT? Certainly not the
excitable young women who make up the ranks of
Lesbian National Parks and Services. Whether
gathering fleshy berries from alpine trails, juicy
peaches from well-groomed orchards or tucking
into ripe melons after a barbeque, Junior Rangers
everywhere love the lusciousness of Nature's bounty,
invariably saying, "More, please!" These active
adventurers can attest that fruit is a delicious part
of any lesbian's diet. However, as naturalists, they
also know that fruit plays an important role in the
sex life of plants, including that of broadleaf trees.

These large, flat-leaved plants are the most
prevalent trees in North America, with over 650
native and naturalized species. Usually deciduous,
they cast off their leaves in the fall and brazenly
flaunt naked branches all winter long. Then, come
spring, they burst into leaf and flower. Some of
their sexual organs (for that is what flowers are) are
small and discreet, like those of the Sugar Maple.
Others are outrageously flamboyant and scream,
"Look at me!" Brightly coloured petals (like those
found on Crabapple, Horse Chestnut, or Hawthorn
trees), or redolent scents (like those found on
Elder, Wild Plum, or Catalpa trees) are two of the
qualities unique to blossoming trees. Like drag

queens and femmes of all persuasions, they know how to arouse interest and produce pleasure.

Broadleaf trees reproduce with the help of a third party, who transfers pollen grains between two plants or from one part of a plant to another. Sometimes this threesome-participant is indifferent to a flower's charms. Gales and gusts, for example, are not susceptible to seduction and so wind-pollinated flowers are often nondescript. However, plants who rely on bats, insects or birds for pollination lure them with bright blooms, tantalizing aroma and sweet nectar. The unwitting participant in plant sex plunges into flower after flower, sometimes hundreds of times a day, to feast on floral juices and, in the process, to deposit heavy pollen grains exactly where the flower wants them.

Some broadleaf trees are called "female" and require genetic material from "male" trees to create seeds; some broadleaf trees are like the conifers and have both "male" and "female" bits, which combine together to ignite the spark of life; and still other broadleafs have both "male" and "female" blooms but cannot self-fertilize, and need material from another tree for reproduction to occur. Be they butch, femme, androgynous or hermaphroditic: it is obvious that the same breadth of diversity exists within the broadleaf sexual community as within our own.

The Sugar Maple
Pride of the "Sugar Bush"

Once egg and pollen cells have joined, seed production begins. Future generations of trees depend on wide distribution of these tiny kernels of life. However, the tree cannot move; she is rooted firmly to the ground. Broadleafs have found ingenious solutions to this problem. Some, like the White Ash and Slippery Elm, create sail-like casings for their seeds, which travel on air currents for great distances. Others, like the Cottonwood, launch each seed with a fluffy parachute. Nut-bearing trees rely on rodents to hide, and forget, their delicious genetic material. The Red Alder, on the other hand, drops its oily, cone-like seeds in rivers and streams, to float downstream to new muddy banks.

The Mountain Ash

Another type of seed distribution is the production of fruit. Fruit-bearers create colourful and delectable seed coats which provide valuable nourishment for animals, birds and insects. Tasty fruits and their seeds are eagerly eaten. However, seeds are not digested, and pass through the bodies of their host to be defecated far and wide. Anal dissemination not only transports the seed to exciting new places, but also provides fertilizer for the nascent sprout.

Over the centuries, gardeners have selectively bred species to enhance their size, texture, flavour and yield of fruit. When Junior Ranger Margo Charlton remembers the dearth of flesh to be found in her 1960s youth, she shudders. But thankfully, that is the past. Due to the work of committed backyard botanists such as herself, there is now plenty of juicy goodness for everyone. "More varieties have come out, and thank Goddess! Plentiful, firm and delicious. And so easy to pick! What more could a homo pomologist ask for?"

Indeed, this gay applebreeder has much to celebrate. Many broadleaf trees, in their quest for propagation, provide us with mouth-watering food value: tender plums, meaty nuts, plump oranges and ripe pears are but a few examples of the harvest which these trees yield. But fruit is only one contribution of broadleaf trees. The stately queens of the forest also give us hardwood, for the manufacture of household articles. They minimize the effects of wind damage and soil erosion, create shade with their leafy boughs and produce an air-conditioning effect through evaporation from their foliage. They are beautiful, to be sure. And to anyone who has climbed a gently curving branch or drunk the intoxicating perfume of blossoms in the spring, a broadleaf tree can be a loyal bowered buddy, a rooted leafy friend.

COMMONLY FOUND SPECIES INCLUDE

apples *(Malus)*	includes all apple and pear varieties
plums *(Prunus)*	Chokecherry, Pembina Plum, Chicksaw Plum, Wild Plum, etc.
oaks *(Quercus)*	White Oak, Bur Oak, Live Oak, Black Oak, Northern Red Oak, etc.
maples *(Acer)*	Sugar Maple, Red Maple, Silver Maple, Box Elder, etc.
elms *(Alnus)*	Red Elm, Mountain Elm, Speckled Elm, etc.
dogwoods *(Cornus)*	Flowering Dogwood, Pacific Dogwood, Red Osier Dogwood, etc.
ashes *(Fraxinus)*	White Ash, Oregon Ash, Green Ash, etc.
basswoods *(Tilia)*	American Basswood, White Basswood, Carolina Basswood, etc.
poplars *(Populus)*	Quaking Poplar, Aspen, Western Cottonwood, etc.
birches *(Betula)*	Grey Birch, Water Birch, Paper Birch, etc.
willows *(Salia)*	Pussy Willow, Pacific Willow, Black Willow, etc.

Palms and Yuccas

LINNAEUS, WHO FIRST developed the system of nomenclature for the biological world, called palms "Princes among plants". Perhaps this is because of their foppish foliage, perhaps because of their primarily bisexual flowers or, perhaps because they are true size queens and possess the largest seeds, longest leaves and largest flower clusters to be found in the plant kingdom. Certainly, they are eccentric. The tropical palms and yuccas are more closely related to grasses than to other flowering tress or conifers. In fact, yuccas are members of the lily family.

These ancient life forms date from the dawn of primates, in the Cretaceous period (70+ million years ago). Their survival is due to their ability to propagate far and wide and endure salty water and windy blasts. Characterized by leaves with parallel veins, they, like many lesbians of southern climes, sport a leathery look. So specialized are their water retention structures that they have unique growth patterns. These large plants, though fibrous, do not have a trunk of wood. However, this is not to imply that they are without integrity. Like many of us, they are simply a little different at their core.

Particularly in the sexual and reproductive realms, these trees show remarkable ingenuity and

The Stately Coconut Palm

have rendered many a lesbian botanist damp with admiration. For example, the Coconut Palm arches over the water and drops its many, football-sized fruits into the briny surf. These fibre-husked seeds float, sometimes for thousands of kilometres, across oceans before being cast upon a sandy shore. Coconut "milk" inside the seed waters and nourishes the young tree as she sprouts. Rich soil and rain are unnecessary. All the nutrients that the young Coconut Palm needs have travelled with her. This adventuress has thus circumnavigated the globe, and can now be found on six continents.

Also called "The Tree of Life", the Coconut is one of the ten most important tree crops in the world. The Coconut is used in the production of many and varied products including macaroons, massage oil, even the medium in which tissue culture is grown. Though not native to North America, the Coconut Palm has thrived on its shores for hundreds of years.

COMMONLY FOUND SPECIES INCLUDE

palms *(Arecaceae or Palmae)*	Royal Palm, Cabbage Palmetto, Washington Palm
yuccas *(Liliaceae)*	Spanish Bayonet, Joshua Tree

Plants

THE PLANT KINGDOM is vast and various, ranging from single-celled species to towering sunflowers. These organisms are divided into six groups to facilitate study. However, plants themselves do not recognize these divisions nor do they accept a hierarchical reading of these groupings. Scientific research supports the fact that many plant types evolved simultaneously and that small or minimalist does not necessarily mean "primitive". Examples of often-scorned plant groups include algae (green, brown and red); parasitic, non-photosynthesizing fungi; mosses and liverworts; clubmosses, horsetails and ferns; and lichens (actually a combination of algae and fungi, locked in an adventuresome, interspecies relationship).

To best serve the active woodswoman, the next pages of this guide will focus on the sixth group, plants with seeds. These species can be divided into two groups: gymnosperms and angiosperms. Gymnosperms, such as the conifers, develop seeds in protective cones. Angiosperms, such as broadleaf trees, produce seed casings which (whether edible or not) we call fruits. Angiosperms include the many wildflowers which grace all North American habitats, from Arctic meadows to rainforest glades, boyish buttonholes to feminine bouquets. It is to these pretty posies that we now turn our gaze . . . .

Wildflowers

When Junior Ranger C.J. Lagartera trudges grey city streets she does not see the social and physical decay that characterize our urban centres. The flotsam and jetsam of consumer society surround her and yet to this blight she is blind. It does not matter to C.J. that this is an urban jungle! She is a junior naturalist! As she wends her way past crack houses, Pizza Huts and parking garages her excitement reaches a fever pitch. Her pencil stands erect at the ready, while her eyes scan the environs. Lips parted with anticipation, she proceeds. J.R. Lagartera knows that natural goodness springs forth from fissures in the pavement and, by gum, she will find it!

C.J. loves wildflowers. If some less enlightened passerby sees the objects of her desire as mere weeds, no matter. For C.J.'s part, all blooms thrill and inspire, and for this love she will make no apology. A diversity of flowers — almost innumerable in hue and shape — burst forth from humble plants. This spectrum forms C.J.'s rainbow flag and she waves it proudly.

Flowers come in every colour imaginable and can be found in even the most inhospitable landscapes, including tundra, deserts and our city cores. These plants are composed of four basic parts: roots, a fleshy stem, leaves and flowers. Like

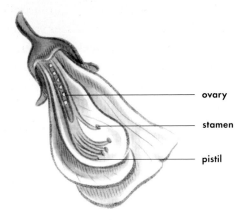

ovary

stamen

pistil

the blossoms of flowering trees, a plant's flower is its showy genital, often luring insects, birds or bats to participate in pollinating threesomes. Genetic material must be transferred from a flower's stamen (made of a filament and an anther) to its pistil (comprised of an erect, clitoral stigma connected to the ovary). Some plants require cross-pollination from other individuals of their species; some plants form seeds by self-pollinating with their own pollen grains.

Flowering plants, or angiosperms, are divided into two groups: monocots and dicots. Monocots, such as grasses, lilies, orchids and tulips, emerge from their seeds as a single leaf. These important plants, which include cereal grains, feed most of the world's *Homo* population. Their long, slender leaves have parallel veins, all of which are attached to the central stem, and their petals usually occur in multiples of three. On the other hand, dicots begin their lives as two leaves which spring from cleft seeds. These plants include peas, beans, potatoes and coffee. Web-like veining marks their branching leaves and flowers usually have four or five uniform petals.

It is important to note that many blooms do not fit neatly into the particulars of this binary. These unique species are J.R. Lagartera's special favourites. Some, like the Pink Ladyslipper, have irregular petals, whereas others, like the Ox-Eye Daisy, are a composite of many tiny flowerets flanked by a ring of ray petals. These plants are not aberrant but simply a variation found within dominant plant culture. No one could accuse the cheery Daisy of being hell-spawn, sick or willfully perverse! She did not choose her composite way of being and, even if she had, her difference has only facilitated her survival and contributed to the wealth of plant life overall.

Some plants, or herbs as they are sometimes called, have evolved defence mechanisms that more than compensate for the vulnerability of their rootedness. The rose and thistle families have thorns which keep interlopers at bay. The Stinging

The Ox-Eye Daisy

Nettle protects itself with thousands of tiny hairs which are filled with an irritating liquid. Poison Ivy and Poison Oak produce an itchy rash. And many, many plants are poisonous to eat. If possible, familiarize yourself with local aggressive or deadly species before trundling off on a hike. Show these plants your respect by avoiding them. Remember, you too have been called "prickly", "thorny", "acrid" and "acerbic" when you wished to be left alone.

These cautions notwithstanding, flowering plants have much to give. With over 250,000 species globally, and probably another 100,000 as yet undiscovered, wildflowers provide something for everyone's tastes. Be it a passive, tree-dwelling Nodding Pogonia Orchid or a bloodthirsty, blood-red Pitcher Plant, herbaceous plant genitals are things of beauty, pleasing pollinators and wayfarers alike. Sadly, it is this very allure that has placed some varieties in jeopardy. Although the idea of picking a flowering lesbian is almost irresistible, Junior Ranger Lagartera and all of us at Lesbian National Parks and Services ask you to exercise restraint. Many of our wildflowers teeter on the brink of extinction. Please, if you must possess your bloom, do so with a camera and leave her physical integrity intact. A deflowered plant cannot bear seeds! Leave the blossoms be. Your mature and selfless act will allow the flower to follow her own path: to grow, propagate and provide enjoyment for generations to come.

Poison Ivy
"If you see leaves of
three, let it be!"

Lesbian National Parks and Services and You!

8

Now that you have acquired a taste for feral lesbianism, perhaps you are wondering what you can do to help. There is so much work that must be done! But really, the most important contribution you can make is an unflinching and vocal commitment to diversity and equality, despite what are often hostile prevailing conditions. Whether you live in a large urban centre or a small rural community, on a mountainside or the vast, open prairie, you can help create a healthier lesbian environment by proudly advocating for a varied natural world. In your words and your deeds, support anomaly and resist the outmoded clap-trap of "normalcy". Wonder, as you wander, not what lesbians can do for you, but what you can do for lesbians.

If you are a true lesbian-lover, you might want to go one step further and consider joining one of the many arms of Lesbian National Parks and Services.

The Lesbian Ranger Corps is a fast-growing and dynamic force of amateurs and professionals dedicated to lesbian wildlife in all its forms. However, the demand for preservation, protection, education and research far outstrips available resources. Lesbian National Parks and Services needs you. Lesbian National Parks and Services wants you. Together we can make a difference.

Becoming A Lesbian Ranger

MANY PEOPLE FANTASIZE about pursuing lesbian-ism full-time. Some are spurred on by "Ranger Envy". They seem to be more interested in wearing the world-famous uniform than in making the deep-seated commitment required to join the Force. Others, more sincere, cannot resist the call-ing of lesbian service. Whatever their motives, these bush enthusiasts offer themselves up on an almost daily basis, asking, "What does it take to become a Ranger?"

Of course this question is not simply answered. Each Ranger is as different from another as one snowflake from the next. However, there are cer-tain features that are essential. A Ranger's sense of duty is her primary characteristic and, in fact, could be described as a defining passion.

To harness the fervour of willing recruits, the Force has developed a rigourous training regime which focuses, first and foremost, upon the preser-vation of lesbian life in all its forms. The aspiring Lesbian Ranger is put through her paces at Training Camp, probing the ins and outs of every lesbian species, from the lowly microbe to the mighty mammal, from the tiny spore to the thrusting oak. Ever cheerful, ever courteous and ever well-pressed, she must be ready at a moment's notice to perform mouth-to-mouth resuscitation or to carry a lesbian casualty to the safety of her base camp. Her every fibre may ache and, occasionally, she may moan, yet the recruit sallies forth, strengthened by the knowledge that her training is an essential step in preparation for a career in lesbianism. Little does she know, the grueling demands of the LNPS Academy (combining physical challenge with hands-on know-how) are nothing compared to the emotional roller coaster she will ride in everyday lesbian life!

Few are called to the Force, and even fewer are able to withstand the pressures of the field. However, those who persevere have truly earned the right to wear the rank bar, "Ranger." Armed with only the LNPS mandate of education, research and recruitment, these intrepid woodswoman will be called upon from dawn to dusk (and well beyond!) to serve and service the lesbian wilds, seven days a week, 24 hours a day. A rousing challenge, to be sure.

Obviously professional lesbianism is not for the faint-of-heart. Those who don the green and tan uniform are embarking upon what is more than a whim, a phase or even a fantasy: they are fulfilling their destiny. The stalwart members of the Force bravely go where no man has gone before, bearing the burden of almost limitless lesbian need. The physical labour alone can leave the Lesbian Ranger

LNPS AND YOU!

spent at day's end! It is deeply gratifying work, but should not be pursued without training or life-long commitment.

Consider this grinding vocation carefully. Try an auxiliary force to test the waters. Then, if you firmly and deeply believe that the world of wrinkle-free polycotton is for you, contact Lesbian Ranger Headquarters to begin the discipline of induction.

Reservists, Available on Demand

Designed to meet the demands of your busy, fast-paced lifestyle, the Lesbian Ranger Reserve offers the flexibility you need and still allows you to serve in times of crisis. Enjoy the camaraderie of monthly meetings, educational retreats and seasonal cook-outs. Impassioned friendships with like-minded folk are a given. Many reservists guiltily admit that they almost hope for a disaster so that they can spend more time with their bosom buddies!

The Reserve Corps is an essential component of the Force and, as a result, requires consummate commitment, albeit part-time. The training period is shorter than for a full-fledged Ranger, but equally intense. Often male members want to join this honed, efficient team, but invariably find aspects of the induction process challenging. However, with unflinching dedication, becoming a Lesbian Ranger Reservist is within everyone's grasp.

Reservists
Buddies in the bush

The Junior Lesbian Ranger Corps

THIS TEAM OF BUDDING women spans the globe, performing good turns and rooting out lesbianism wherever potential lurks. The Junior Lesbian Rangers come from all walks of life and are all ages, but share a common thirst for each other. By working together, righting wrongs and wearing uniforms, they have made an important contribution to environmental conservation the world over. The impact this corps has had on lesbian proliferation is indisputable, as is the satisfaction its members have garnered from their labour of love. Naturally, this feeling of accomplishment breeds increased self-esteem and self-confidence. When considered together with the vigourous (almost relentless!) exercise of mind and body, the Junior Lesbian Ranger Corps is one of the most healthful leadership programs developed to date.

To become a Junior Lesbian Ranger, one must undergo a strict induction process under the supervision of an older or more experienced lesbian. This training is extensive, and includes mastery of many skills necessary to lesbian life. To receive a more detailed description of these rigours, order the Junior Ranger Handbook, available for $14 CDN (postage included) from LNPS Headquarters, 485 Wardlaw Ave., Winnipeg, Manitoba, Canada R3L 0L9. This handy

Official Junior Ranger Crest

reference illustrates a plethora of wilderness tips, as well as advice on how to move an insensible lesbian and care for her wounds and vulnerable body parts. Many a Junior Ranger, thinking herself adept in the bush, has been humbled by the wealth of information provided by this slim tract and has wished that all women were provided with the intimate knowledge its pages so succinctly provide.

The Handbook also contains the Anthem of the Junior Lesbian Ranger, a hymn which swells the hearts and loins of all who hear its glad refrain. Sung by a chorus of lusty voices, the Anthem embodies the joie de vivre of outdoor fun which the Corps is so happy to provide.

PLEDGE OF
THE JUNIOR LESBIAN RANGER

I promise to do my duty:
       to lesbian wildlife
       and the sisterhood of the Force.

I promise to be visible:
       on the trails
       and on the streets.

I promise to be courteous:
       to be clean
       and well-pressed.

But most of all, I promise to be kind,
       to maintain good posture
       and in spite of all adversity
       to sing, smile and be gay.

Maintaining Order in the Wilds

ONE OF THE DUTIES of the Lesbian Ranger is to ensure that neither lesbians nor their environments are directly threatened. This is not always the most pleasant duty. Heterosexual interlopers, usually bi-ped and travelling in pairs, pose the greatest challenge. Despite our distaste and the obvious risks involved, it is essential that these organisms be rebuffed. Ultimately, ignorance and indifference must be replaced with enlightenment and appreciation, so that lesbian ecosystems can remain unscathed.

In order to more effectively fight this battle, the Force has developed a ticketing system to punish violators. We invite you to reproduce this form (see overleaf), and to perform citizen arrests when necessary. As you will note, tickets can be issued to lesbians as well. "Flirtation without intent," for example, is a frequent lesbian failing, as is, on occasion, "Inappropriate footwear." Although Lesbian National Parks and Services is not mandated to police lesbian behaviour, we do believe that all of us should be encouraged to be the best that we can be.

Socks with Sandals
A frequent error

LNPS AND YOU!

259

Violations
You are hereby deputized to
issue tickets to miscreants.
Please cut out this form, copy
and distribute when necessary.

VIOLATION

THE FOLLOWING has committed a violation in contravention of the rules and regulations of **Lesbian National Parks and Services**:

NAME　　　　　　　　　　　　　　　　DATE

		FINE
INAPPROPRIATE FOOTWEAR	☐	$50
INAPPROPRIATE HETEROSEXUAL BEHAVIOUR	☐	$100
OFFENSIVE T-SHIRT	☐	$50
FLIRTATION WITHOUT INTENT	☐	$100
FAILURE TO RESPOND TO A RANGER'S AUTHORITY	☐	$100
FEEDING THE LESBIAN WILDLIFE	☐	$50
OTHER　☐ $50　☐ $100　☐ $250	☐	$500

AUTHORIZED BY　　　　　　　　　　LOCATION

PLEASE REMIT PAYMENT TO **LESBIAN NATIONAL PARKS AND SERVICES HEADQUARTERS**
485 WARDLAW AVENUE, WINNIPEG, MANITOBA, CANADA R3L 0L9

Conclusion

9

WE HOPE YOU HAVE enjoyed the wonders of lesbian wildlife and survival as experienced through the pages of this book. This is a burgeoning field being expanded daily, thanks to committed amateur naturalists such as yourselves. Please continue to conduct your own research and share it freely with others. Your generosity will be rewarded many times over, for you will have contributed to a happy, healthy ecosystem for all.

Fortunately, some very good texts exist to further enlighten the reader. The most exhaustive work to date on homosexuality in animals is Bruce Bagemihl's *Biological Exuberance*. Although we did not draw upon this tome in writing our volume (preferring our own first-hand field experience), we most heartily recommend it. Otherwise, any well-researched volume will provide sufficient detail from which a dogged lesbian can extrapolate. *The Larousse*

Encyclopedia of Animal Life and Alex Bristow's *The Sex Life of Plants* are both thorough and intellectually arousing. For an analysis of the mistakes and omissions which scientific naming has wrought, a fellow Canadian, Marc Ereshefsky, and his book *The Poverty of The Linnaean Hierarchy*, lead the field.

Bigotry, and especially heterosexism, have led to many omissions in the field of natural science which must be righted and redressed. This daunting task will be achieved only through the efforts of many hands working together in concert. Fortunately you, dear reader, probably have two such appendages, which can be applied ably to lesbians in need. Whether your adventures in biology take you to the library, the climax forest or the bedroom, never stint on dexterity. Manual skills, when combined with curiosity and courage, will serve you well. As you bravely tromp carpeted hallways or virgin terrain, always queery, "Where are the lesbians?" and "How can I get one?". Remember, we are an exciting and excited part of Nature's bounty and contribute to the essence of species survival: diversity.

Acknowledgements

A RESEARCH PROJECT of this magnitude is not possible without the labour and enthusiasm of many committed bush-lovers. Lesbian National Parks and Services would like to express its sincerest gratitude to the many, many people who contributed to this book. In particular we would like to thank Carol Philipps, Maxine Hasselriis and Milada Kováčová for their tireless pursuit of errant commas, mysterious meanings and unlikely words. *Artistes par excellence* Daniel Barrow, Noreen Stevens and Zab deserve special merit badges in the field of "Good Grooming" as they have toiled above and beyond the call of duty, ensuring that this book looks its best. Our publisher, Beth Follett (Junior Ranger Feral Girl), has been a patient and kind task-mistress. She deserves high praise and heart-felt thanks for her dedication to producing the finest book we could muster. Finally, we extend our warmest thank you to all those Junior Rangers, from the youngest to the oldest, the smallest to the largest, from all across the globe and right here at home, who are the backbone of the Force, inspiring us in all that we do. We salute you!

ACKNOWLEDGEMENTS

ABOUT THE AUTHORS

Lesbian Rangers Shawna Dempsey and Lorri Millan founded Lesbian National Parks and Services in 1997 and have been vigilantly probing lesbian wildlife ever since. Their tours-of-duty in ecosystems as diverse as Banff National Park, Michigan Women's Big Game Park and Sydney's Gay and Lesbian Mardi Gras have turned quite a few heads, and ultimately garnered the Rangers international respect for their deep-seated commitment to the lesbian wilds. Dempsey and Millan's pioneering efforts in the fields of conservation and preservation have also inspired others, and many have joined the Junior Lesbian Ranger Corps, a worldwide organization devoted to lesbiancraft and outdoor fun. Despite the rigours of the LNPS vocation — which includes the perils and rewards of active recruitment — Dempsey and Millan find time for hobbies as fascinating and varied as performance art and experimental video. In or out of uniform, the dogged duo call Winnipeg, Manitoba, Canada, headquarters and home.